NATURAL SELECTION

(a novel by James Walker)

Dedicated to the crew of the U.S.S. Patriot...

CONTENTS:

PREFACE 9
Chapter 1 15
Chapter 2 31
Chapter 3 41
Chapter 4 47
Chapter 5 54
Chapter 6 62
Chapter 7 64
Chapter 8 70
Chapter 9 79
Chapter 10 85
Chapter 11 90
Chapter 12 96
Chapter 13 109
Chapter 14 114
Chapter 15 124
Chapter 16 130
Chapter 17 140
Chapter 18 145
Chapter 19 153
Chapter 20 159
Chapter 21 165
Chapter 22 169
Chapter 23 174
Chapter 24 180
Chapter 25 188
Chapter 26 190
Chapter 27 195
Chapter 28 202

PREFACE:

Back in 1993 I saw Tom Hanks star in a movie called *"Philadelphia."* I had known about AIDS for over ten years, but it wasn't till I saw that film did I really think about the human suffering that attaches itself to those stricken with the illness. As someone who grew up and lives in the *Bible Belt,* it doesn't surprise me that back in the 80's I heard people claiming that *AIDS was a plague God had sent down upon the homosexuals.* However, it did surprise me when an African-American friend of mine told me that he believed the AIDS virus was a conspiracy by the government to do away with *minorities.*

Even back then I considered *both scenarios rather ridiculous.* However, I was very much intrigued with the second premise as a plot device for a novel. At first, I imagined a government conspiracy like my friend had suggested, but rejected that for two reasons. One... it is very obvious to me that Congress has difficulty agreeing on relatively benign courses of action, let alone something as grandiose as a *covert surgical genocide.* And I don't believe something like that could ever be kept secret... *soon or later it would leak out.* The other reason was I really liked the idea of a *mad scientist on a mission.* I have always admired what I call, *scientific entrepreneurs* like: Edison, Tesla or the Wright Brothers. ***I wanted a twisted version of someone like that.***

Although my Dr. Noah Little is sort of an anti-hero, he does bring up things we as a society should be thinking about: like over population; or the wisdom of financing social programs that economies can not support, benefiting people who abuse the systems and essentially take the bread out of the mouths of the middle class; and of course, the damage drug abuse is doing to our prodigy both physically and culturally.

Another thing I hope my little story will lift up is that

even though it seems that the AIDS epidemic has stepped out of the limelight of the world stage, it has by no means ceased to be a problem. So far, the number of people who have died from AIDS related illnesses is a number equal to almost half the population of Great Britain.... *and the death toll continues.*

Noah Little's answers to the world's problems is rather *like throwing the baby out with the bath water,* but he looks at problems we don't think about. And although I have taken poetic license with a few things to tell a good story, I hope my character will inspire people to take a hard look at the way we live our lives in the respect so few of us even think about, let alone plan for future generations.

If we don't change that attitude .... *Noah Little may not be so wrong in the way he looks at things.*

On April 24th, 1980, Ken Horne, a resident of San Francisco becomes the first recognized case of AIDS in the United States ....

On October 31st,1980, a French-Canadian flight attendant by the name of Gaëtan Dugas pays his first known visit to New York City bathhouses. He would later be called *"Patient Zero"* for his apparent connection to many early cases of AIDS in the United States.....

On December 23rd 1980, a Brooklyn school teacher by the name of Rick Wellikoff becomes the 4th American to have died from AIDS....

It is estimated in the United States that more than a million people are living with HIV and more than a half a million people have died after developing AIDS since the 1980's.....

In 2009 it was estimated globally there are between 31 and 35 million people living with HIV/AIDS ...

Since the beginning of the epidemic, nearly 30 million people have died from AIDS-related causes....

And so far ....*there is no cure.*

CHAPTER ONE

August 17ᵗʰ, 1979

Noah Little was wringing wet when he sprang upright in his tousled little bed, awakened by yet another nightmare. He looked around the ragged, dingy, flophouse room, straining to focus on its crude furnishings illuminated by the dim light of the dusk city skyline. He could hear the faint muffled sound of someone's stereo obliquely blaring from one of the rooms upstairs, but could only make out a sketch of the booming bass line. Ten stories below, a siren screamed by; faint at first... Doppler shift; then a slow diminishing whisper, lost in the normal collage of sounds made by many moving vehicles along a metropolitan avenue. His neighbors to the left side were having a heated argument, while in the apartment adjacent to his bedstead, a couple were violently having sex, punctuated by all the grunts and groans that usually go along with the act. Their bed bumped up against the wall with such force that it made the framed, faded pictures on his side rattle softly with each stroke.

Noah groggily staggered to his feet, walked across the room and snapped on its only source of artificial lighting - a single, naked, 60 watt bulb. The old derelict wearily padded into the bathroom, pulled the chain dangling from a florescent light fixture, turning it on, and bathing the room with bluish-white light. The room reeked profusely of urine, made worse by the August heat and humidity; the pungency so severe it all but masked the stench of his own musty body odor.

Noah Little studied the image in the medicine cabinet mirror. *"Were those the eyes of a cold blooded killer?"* he asked himself inwardly. *"They must be,"* he mused, for he had killed, and in cold blood, even though he had rationalized his reasons many times. He wondered at the bloodshot gray eyes staring blankly back at him. If they were the eyes of a killer, at what point did they become so? Was it when he had become a murderer, or *were they always so?* Did their gaze shimmer even as a child with the evil predestination of one who would take life? Noah did not know. Now, the sunken hollow eyes merely looked sad.

When he had gone back into the other room he sat down at a small desk and pulled out a package of cigarettes from the center drawer. He lit up, exhaled loudly, then watched the ringlets of smoke float in the air in front of him. He consulted his wristwatch: 7:45 P.M. eastern daylight savings time. It was almost time to go to work; *to tend the garden,* as he would call it.

His mother had had a garden, about a half an acre almost: a garden under a grand blue mid-western sky beneath a big bright country sun. When he had been a boy he had helped her plant it, harvest it... *and weed it.* The latter of which, she did with a vengeance. She hated weeds. Beyond their obvious drawbacks - choking the harvest, the backbreaking toil needed to remove them, etc. - it was the very concept of weeds that disgusted her most. In her view, weeds were big, ugly, useless brutes that stole the very life blood from the noble vegetables, whose lives were infinitely more important. But all of that had been so long ago... a lifetime ago. *Still, how much of that simple philosophy had dominated the shape of his destiny?* Could that small page out of his childhood have been the embryo, or *seed,* to extend the metaphor, for the eyes of a killer staring back at him almost a half century later? *Possibly.*

Noah thought of Minnesota. The world had been so small when he had lived there. He had been so innocent then; clean, fresh, not this morose husk he had become. He had been so at peace then, before all the notions and intellectualizing had perverted the way he saw that innocence into something he had for so many years loathed, but now, ironically longed for.

*"People are too aware. They think too much. Their lives have to have some purpose to mean anything; not like animals. Dogs live solely for the sake of living. They live just for what the good Lord rains down on all of us: the warm sunshine, a cool breeze when it's hot, an afternoon nap, good food, good friends... **and a good screw**,"* his father had once told him on a lazy summer afternoon while stroking the head of an ancient beagle in their back yard in Minnesota.

Noah's father had been a veterinarian in a rural community near a small town called, Larson. It was from him that Noah first gained an appreciation for life, and the delicate balance of nature. His father looked at creation as a song sung by a symphony: harmonies playing against melodies, rhythms, crescendos, pianissimos. Even now, after all that had happened, Noah still shared his dead father's summation of the cosmos - but with a few amendments. Chief of these amendments to the celestial symphony was that care must be taken to not let harmony overrun melody, lest the masterpiece degrade into chaotic noise.

*****

Noah Little stripped off his yellowing, sweat stained tank-top undershirt and boxer shorts, and then stepped into the shower. The water felt good against his skin. When he had finished the shower, he stood nude before the cabinet mirror, his discarded clothing lying in a heap next to the toilet. Once again he considered his haggard 52 year old face as he began to lather it in preparation for shaving. *How long did he have left?* Two years, three, he guessed. Soon, he would not physically be able to carry on his work. Maybe when he retired he'd go back to Minnesota for his last days. *"Retirement,"* he mused, and rather warmed to the notion of calling it that.

He went back to the bedroom, took semi-clean underwear from a severely scarred and scratched chest of drawers, and a semi-clean change of clothes from the closet, then dressed while mildew grew in the wet shower.

When he had dressed he pulled a frazzled old suitcase from underneath the bed, opened it, and then removed a false bottom. Under the false bottom was 30 thousand dollars in large bills. He had two larger suitcases such as this one. One was locked in an airport locker with 210 thousand inside; the other, locked in a bus station locker with 150 thousand. He kept the money at the egresses of the city so he could make a quick get-a-way if he were to be found.

How much would he need tonight?... fifty dollars? a hundred?...two?... sometimes it was expensive. If he felt up to it he might even do two jobs tonight; after all, *it was his birthday.*

When he hit the streets he contemplated the hard faces of the urban jungle that paraded before him. They looked so much like the faces of the patients he had treated during his intern days at the E.R.

*****

When *Dr. Noah Jonas Little* graduated from medical school, he was brimming over with enthusiasm, wanting to alleviate the suffering of his fellow man. By his second year of residence, his patients were just so many dumb animals who lacked the good sense to stay out of the highway. It seemed the horrible predicaments they got themselves into on close examination turned out to be a direct result of their own wretched stupidity, and no matter how many times they got burned, they never learned anything. Noah found himself treating the same man over and over for practically the same thing again and again. Towards the end of his residency he had completely lost his fire. He would do a competent job, but nothing more. Casualties of gang wars would come and go everyday. If he saved a man's life, the bloody idiot would just go out and get himself shot again the next week. *And over what?* Because he defiantly walked down a slum squalor street claimed by a rival warring tribe of adolescent metropolitan Neanderthals. *Better he die and get it over with and not waste good bandages.*

Finally, Noah began to feel he had chosen the wrong profession, so he quit the hospital, moved back to Minnesota, and worked about a year or so for his father's veterinary practice.

*****

Derelict Noah Jonas Little sat down on a street bench and watched the early evening traffic bustle by. He lit another cigarette and pondered his bleak future. *Would he go to hell?* **Probably.** But was not what he was doing for *a greater good? And was not he giving up his life for others?* He flashed on a Sunday school teacher he had had when he was ten years old. His teacher had quoted the Holy Scriptures: "No greater love haveth a man than he who would lay down his life for his friends..." *Isn't that what he had done?*

And what about the people he had killed? Usually they were such a miserable lot. *What prospects had they? What would they do with their lives but raise up another generation who would be just as useless as themselves: breeding like rabbits, eating up precious raw materials and speeding up the entropy of the human race?*

Yes, what he was doing was right, he kept telling himself. Still, why did sleep so often elude him, and when he did manage brief periods of unconsciousness, why was it invaded by such hideous nightmares? *Guilty?* "*Could that have been the way it had been for the hiding Nazi war criminals?"* Noah asked himself. But he wasn't like them. Of course, couldn't they have sported similar reasons for the horrors they committed? *"Yes, but they were insane,"* he thought to himself, and then asked, *"If I had gone mad somewhere along the way would I be aware of it?"* The question laid heavy on his mind.

He took a puff off the cigarette, changing the subject of his mental conversation. *He remembered little Tyrone.* Noah had been doing a fourteen hour shift in the E.R. back during his intern days, when a very weary looking social worker had brought him in. He was a cute little kid; all of seven years, wet tears streaming down his light brown African-American face.

*****

"Where's it hurt, little guy?" Noah asked, heart almost breaking with sympathy. Little Tyrone didn't speak, didn't sob, he just sat there on the examination table staring at Noah with tiny tears draining from tortured puppy dog eyes.

When Noah finished his examination he found that Tyrone's teeth had never seen a toothbrush, and some of the cavity laden teeth had decayed to the point of abscess. The infection had spread along his jawbone into his ears, rupturing the eardrums, and killing the auditory nerves. *Now, the child would be forever deaf as a stone.*

Searing anger burned at Noah's very soul till it erupted out his mouth like hot lava from an active volcano. "Son of a bitch! Son of a bitch! Nurse! Where in the fuck is this little boy's mamma?"

The timid little nurse blinked in startled bewilderment. Noah walked over to her, then leaning over her slight figure, stopping mere inches from her face, snapped, "Well, speak up woman!"

"I - I - I don't know, Doctor," came her reply as she stepped back a few paces in retreat.

"Well, get the lead outta your lard ass and find out... STAT!"

The nurse was frozen with fear, unable to move.

"Now, dammit!" the young doctor barked.

That broke her free. She scurried off to do what Noah had commanded.

When Noah found Tyrone's mother, his verbal assault was so severe, the shear volume of the words almost drew blood.

"...What sorta crazy bitch are you?" he screamed the question at a frightened little black woman. She was a short squat creature with a two year old on one hip and two more toddlers slightly older standing to either side. All stared wide-eyed and unmoving, like animals frozen by the headlights of an oncoming car.

"What were you thinking?" Noah went on rapid fire: "For cryin' out loud, woman, there's gotta be a hundred and sixty dentists in this town and a half a dozen free clinics. The least you could have done was bought the child a fuckin' toothbrush. What is wrong with you? That child in there is going to live the rest of his life in a world without sound and there's not one damn good reason for it! Are you stupid or can't you keep your panties on long enough to look after your own kids? And what the hell are you doing with four kids anyway? Haven't you ever heard of birth control? Didn't you ever think about the responsibility you would have to them before you stuck your legs up in the air? They deserve better than you. A damn dog deserves better than you! Lady you oughta be locked up for what you've done!"

At this point all four were in tears, babies sobbing, and the whole crowded waiting room sat agog at the spectacle playing before them. Then suddenly, Noah felt the social worker pulling on one arm and the head physician on the other.

"Doctor, I think you need to settle down," an appalled Dr. Peter Gates warned. "Go back in the lounge and cool off, Noah."

Noah realized that he had lost it, and felt a tinge of embarrassment, but still his emotions were not anywhere near being under control. Going to the lounge was probably a very good career move. He still had enough presence of mind to realize that, so he jerked away from the both of them and stormed through the hall to plop down in the doctor's lounge like a misbehaving child who had been sent to his room.

"How could anyone be so irresponsible?" he asked himself. But yet, she was hardly more than a child herself: barely twenty. "You have to have a license to practice medicine, you have to have a license to drive a car... you even have to have a license to catch a fish for Pete's sake! Why in the hell don't you have to have a license to bring children into the world?" he lamented out loud.

Noah got up and got himself a cup of black coffee from a row of vending machines along the lounge wall, then sat back down at the table. He stared blankly into the cup, turning things over in his mind for a long time. Suddenly, a knock on the open door distracted him. It was the social worker. She had been pretty once, now, she had a weather-beaten countenance, possibly brought on by her profession. She was about forty-five with large dark eyes framed by crow's feet. Her hair was gray, speckled with black streaks here and there: her frame, slightly plump.

"That was quite a show, Doctor," she said coolly.

Noah's features hardened, but he said nothing.

"Well... I'm glad you said what you did, because if you hadn't, I probably would have."

She sat down opposite him, her dark eyes looking directly into his, conveying understanding. She paused a moment, then continued, "But it wouldn't have done any good. Latosha, bless her heart, the girl tries but she's as dumb as a rock. I know there's been times I've wanted to give her a swift kick myself, but when you kick a rock, *all you do is stub your toe.*"

Noah looked back into his coffee cup. He searched for the words to express the tornado of righteous indignation which whirled in his mind, but now that the adrenaline had worn off, the best he could do was croak out in a papery voice, "Why?"

The woman sighed and looked down at Noah's cup as if it might have been a crystal ball into the man's soul. "That's a good one, Doc. There is *no why*, there just *is.* All we can do is salvage what we can from each situation.

I've seen a hundred kids like Latosha Manns. Latosha had Tyrone when she was fourteen years old. She quit school when she was in the seventh grade - just as well, she hardly ever went anyway. So, its little wonder she reads on a third grade level. Her father was murdered when she was four. Her stepfather raped her when she was ten. Her mother is a *cokehead.* And now, Latosha is a third generation welfare recipient. Let's face it, the child doesn't have a whole lot to work with, so you really can't expect a whole lot from her."

Noah looked at the social worker, his anger diminishing, and said shaking his head slowly, "One man's family."

"Yeah."

"It's all so senseless...so...*so hopeless.*"

"Senseless, yes - *hopeless?* Not quite. Every now and then the good guys win. You gotta hang in there for the times when you can make a difference."

"But that's gotta be few and far in between. What does any of it matter?"

"It matters a whole hellva lot to *the few and the far in between.*"

But Noah could never see it that way. He began to see his role in the world as a losing proposition at best and a total waste of time at worst. Something deep inside Noah changed after Tyrone. From that point on, he never quite saw people as human beings. All he saw were.... *vegetables and weeds.*

*****

Noah Little tossed the cigarette butt on the sidewalk next to the bench where he sat and regarded the prostitutes on post just ahead of him. He had had whores all over the world. He liked English tarts best. French and German whores were too hairy for his taste. American working girls came across as more of a commercial venture. They had a product to sell and put their goods up front for all to see in an open air exhibition while they barked a sales pitch. And like all good entrepreneurs know, packaging is everything. For example, if the call girl in question had large breasts, the neckline plunged, if the derriere was shapely, butt cheeks hung out both sides of short shorts. If she was not particularly striking, the idea was to wear outrageous wigs and as little clothing as one could wear without being completely naked.

"Which one would it be?" he asked himself. None of the four prostitutes struck his fancy. He decided to walk

on. There would certainly be lots to choose from. *After all, it was his birthday.*

*****

Towards the end of his second year of residency Dr. Noah Little, M.D. had had his fill of urban medicine, so he packed up and moved back home to Minnesota, where he for all intents and purposes, became a veterinary assistant. His father didn't exactly know how to take his son's career detour, especially taking account for the obscenely large amount of money which had been expended for his medical education. The senior Dr. Little didn't press too hard the issue however, because one, he tended to be supportive of his children to a blind fault, and two, he had strongly advised Noah to follow in his footsteps, and now it seemed, (if rather belatedly) he was about to do just that.

During that summer, a violent epidemic of hoof and mouth disease broke out among the local herds which had everyone completely baffled. Apparently, the strain had mutated into something which the local veterinary community found much to their chagrin, to be totally impervious to all conventional treatments. Cattle were dropping like flies. It was in the midst of that event that Noah found his true calling as a research scientist. After extensive field and lab work, the young medical doctor astounded his elder colleagues by actually developing a viable vaccine that effectively counteracted the rampaging cattle disease.

While he was doing the afore mentioned field work Noah met and soon fell in love with a quite charming, and uncommonly handsome young woman, who had found herself employed as a waitress at a rural eating establishment known far and wide simply as *Ray's*. The curvaceous redhead took night classes at Larson Community College in secretarial sciences, and was full of dreams about becoming a high level executive secretary and using that position to marry well.

Noah would come in from the cow pastures for lunch, and she would keep his coffee cup full while he poured over his research notes from that morning's field work, spread out over the back table that he would convert into a desk. They were married in the fall and some time later had a child who died when she was two. The young woman was *Marie*.

Noah attracted a modest notoriety in scientific circles, but anything but modest compensation from a major animal pharmaceutical company for his hoof and mouth vaccine. A year after his marriage to Marie he was very nearly a millionaire, and soon shifted back into human medicine, eventually doing cancer research at several large northwestern universities. Part of his duties placed him in teaching roles, and as a myriad of professorships came and went, he became a fine teacher while his career moved him around the country. Towards the twilight of that career he landed positions at such prestigious schools as *Cal Tech, Harvard Medical School*, and lastly, the *Cambridge School of Internal Medicine,* at Cambridge, England.

Dr. Little enjoyed his laurels. He had become a respected man in his field, and he was also quite proud of the breakthrough cancer research he had accomplished. In a relatively short time his success inflated his ego beyond self-importance and arrogance, to the very brink of megalomania.

Noah Little enjoyed the university environment. Mostly he relished always being surrounded by sagely faculty and his quick-witted graduate and under graduate students, all of which respected him highly, some bordering on *hero worship*. The people he dealt with were always extremely bright, intelligent and highly motivated.

The opposition to the clientele of his earlier medical career was so striking it seemed to take on an almost surreal timbre; almost as if it had been a part of someone else's life.

At any rate, the chasm between *Noah Little, world renowned scientist,* and *Noah Little, E.R. intern* seemed great most of the time. However, it seemed very small when dealing with his wife. Despite the fact that he fancied himself a member of an elite scholarly aristocracy, he could not escape his growing estimation of his wife as a peasant of the most rude variety. She was an anchor to his middle class heritage, and brought back with vivid clarity all the ignorance, absurdity, and futility he had so abhorred while an intern.

As for Marie, she did love her husband, always did, and always would, but loved his *money* much, much more. And Dr. Little's success did generate lots of money. Marie had ascended from the most modest of backgrounds, and her husband's wealth grew to more than she could have ever imagined, so naturally, she soon became a shining example to all the world of *the epitome of the novo riche.* She spent money in the most gaudy ways possible, and there was always more coming in, in seeming inexhaustible supplies.

This spending seemed such an ugly thing to Noah. She accomplished nothing but a collection of cars, shoes, clothing, furniture and whatnots. And even though she had enough trinkets and shiny baubles for any ten women, her prime motivation in life seemed to be the acquisition of more. Noah soon began to see that the mind of the woman he had married was no match for the beautiful body to which it was attached. Marie, although bright and reasonably intelligent, never applied herself, nor strove to be or do anything. This trait, added to the other ways both she and Noah had changed with his success, soon made for a doomed marriage.

When Little came home in the evenings he soon became quite adept at tuning out his wife. To his ears she was constantly babbling incoherently about things which appeared to him to be so trivial they really didn't warrant his attention. He would adopt the distracted posture of a weary parent, pretending to listen to a two year old, occasionally interjecting a groan or grunt from time to time; feigning interest. Fortunately, Marie's recitations required very little in the way of interaction.

As years went by, from time to time his irritation would peak and he would snap at her coldly. This eventually evolved into verbal, and then into physical abuse. After such episodes she would recoil briefly, but after he had cooled off, all was forgiven.

She was like a drug addict. She would endure any insult or humiliation, for her insecurity bordered on paranoia. She would not do anything which would remotely put her access to the money in jeopardy. Although, she did have one weapon in her defense arsenal, and she wielded it like *Excalibur* - **she was a thunder in bed!**

Little was perfectly cognizant of the situation, and cursed himself for his weakness. He knew he was sexually dependent on the voluptuous redhead, and it caused him more than a little self-reproach that she had such control over his baser instincts. He also knew she was a *money addict,* and would endure practically anything as long as he fed her habit. So, he rationalized his dependency on her purely as a bodily function, like defecation or urination, and thusly often treated her like a toilet or a urinal. Most of the time, he exhibited no respect for his wife as a sentient soul. *He saw her as a weed, his weed, but a weed nonetheless.*

When they had a child Noah began to have more human feelings for his wife. Marie almost died giving birth, so, perhaps, his opinion of her improved out of guilt.

Perhaps, the arrival of *Mandy Marie Little*, softened the stony heart of the now, nearly emotionless scientist. But whatever it was, the child was a joy to both of them and Noah lost a lot of his cynicism and arrogance. For two years the three of them lived a happy life.

Then came tragedy. Marie was driving home from Larson, where she and Mandy had spent the Memorial Day weekend visiting her parents, when she was run off the road by a drunk driver. Professor Little had elected not to join them for the holiday, as he was in the midst of an experiment which he did not want to leave unattended. When the state police notified him of the accident he rushed to the hospital to find that Marie had suffered a shattered leg and pelvis, and his daughter Mandy had been killed instantly. Afterward he grieved pitifully for a month. The couple tried to have more children, but it was discovered that the crash had left Marie sterile. Through all of this the remaining humanity drained away from the young professor, and Noah Little... *became an evil man.*

With Mandy dead Noah reverted back to his former cycle of abuse. Now, he became almost sadistic. There were times when Marie was afraid he would kill her; *and justly so.* Fourteen long years passed, and no one ever suspected the Nobel laureate of the horrible secret life he led behind the manicured lawns of his mansions. No one noticed how Mrs. Little often seemed to use an awful lot of make up, and how she seemed to miss a lot of faculty functions. *Dr. Little's wife sure was a frail creature*, often contracting various illnesses requiring protracted periods of convalescence. *How fortunate it must be for her to be married to a man who among other things was a medical doctor...* **No one knew the truth.**

Then one day there was one too many arguments, one too many black eyes and one too many swollen lips. The humiliation and degradation finally outweighed Marie's fear of being cut off from the money, and she filed for divorce... *and won an overwhelming victory in the settlement.*

Although Little had plenty of money, the resentment he felt when he sent her the huge alimony checks each month quickly matured into vile disgust, then into savage and putrid hatred.

*****

Noah Little thought of his former wife that hot August evening as he strolled along the city streets looking for a whore. *"That's all right, bitch! I fixed your little wagon,"* he said aloud under his breath, as a wry smile crossed his thin lips. The smell of cooked onions captured his attention as he passed a greasy spoon (slash) pool hall and bar, making him realized that he was hungry.

He went in and ordered a couple of hot dogs and a beer. As he ate he watched the patrons across the room playing pool under a colorful stained glass light fixture made to resemble a beer bottle. The sound of the cue ball striking the other billiard balls *time warped his remembrances back twenty seven years.*

CHAPTER TWO

The cue ball struck the triangle of multi-colored spheres, sending them scurrying around the green surface of Alec Grand's billiard table. *Medical student Noah Little* rubbed blue chalk from a small cube in his right hand onto his cue stick, as the steady tic-tock of the grandfather's clock marked time behind him.

"All I'm saying is that mankind has perverted the natural order of the earth," Dr. Grand announced.

"I can't see it that way. It's... it's more like he's cultivated a wilderness. That's not perversion," countered Noah.

"How long has man been on the scene? ...100 thousand years?...150?...200 thousand if you stretch it? That's a grain of sand in the hourglass of time. If you ask me the earth got along a lot better before it was... *cultivated* ...with industrial waste, atomic fallout, and sanitary landfills."

"Dr. Grand, I concede that mankind has not been a good steward of the earth, but I believe that if there is a quote, unquote, *'grand cosmic scheme'*, man evolved to have dominion over the earth so that he could develop the things that really count: art, philosophy, science, literature, mathematics... To accomplish all of this he had to have an environment sufficiently challenging enough to lead him to experimentation, and as the ages rolled by meeting those challenges provided two things: A) control of that environment freeing him for B), the acquisition of understanding and intellectual pursuit. The prowess for the first effectively equipping him for the latter."

With that Noah took a shot, sinking the 7 ball in the corner pocket, while Grand digested what he had said.

"So, bottom line what you're saying is that God created the whole of the natural world so that man would evolve a technology advanced enough to build a city in which John Steinbeck could be born and educated, so he could grow up and write The *Grapes Of Wrath*."

"Well, uh... mmm I suppose that's basically the gist of it, yes."

"The big problem I have with all that Noah, is that you are putting man outside the natural world. You've got him pragmatically in control of nature. This evades the basic fact that man is an animal, and is driven by the same primal motivations as a saber tooth tiger: to eat, dominate and *fuck*."

"This is true, but in time we will evolve out of our carnal cradle. It will take time, sure. As you say we as a race have only been here but a single grain in the temporal hourglass, but think how far we've come since the caves, and imagine what we'll become in say, the next 50 thousand years."

Dr. Grand sank the last remaining ball into the side pocket, stood up, and walked over to the bar to refill his bourbon glass. "You're still denying the basic laws of nature; making man outside the natural world, but rather he is but a small part of it. Man doesn't control nature; *he is controlled by it*.

Would you like a refill?"

Noah handed his glass to Grand, and as he filled it with scotch and soda, went on with his debate. "On the contrary, is it not a basic law of nature that all things evolve? What I'm suggesting is the logical progression of man's natural evolution. When he left the caves he had to evolve from a hunter-gather, to a farmer, then to a technology wielding creature. As he passed through all these stages he took things he had learned from the lower levels, and combined them with new things, then discarded things that were obsolete. The logical evolutionary progression must one day land him into an Olympian utopia where his carnal needs become obsolete."

"...Damn, you are an optimistic bastard, aren't you?"

Noah smiled, and then teacher and student exited Grand's billiard room/den carrying their drinks onto a patio via two French doors, and sat down in black wrought iron chairs.

Grand took a sip from his drink and continued, "Noah, I disagree with your scenario. You have everything evolving into infinity. For everything there is a season. Everything dies. It's a part of life. It's as much a part of the elemental laws of the universe as gravity. Look around you..." Grand pointed up into the starry, moonless night sky. "Every one of those stars will one day burn out. *Nothing*, absolutely nothing in the physical universe is permanent. Everything has a finite existence."

"I'm well acquainted with the concept of entropy, Dr. Grand, but we are dealing with enormously long periods of time here. I can't subscribe to the fatalist viewpoint."

"*Fatalist?* Ah, the innocence of youth. Noah, you'll make a fine doctor one day, but mark my words, you will at some point in your life become a member of that contemptible society of *fatalists*, but on that day you will call yourself a *realist*.

I'm not saying that we should kick up our feet, roll over and die. No, far from it. Life is the most precious of all gifts, and the potentials and possibilities are staggering. But neither is it a story without end. I agree we are speaking of extraordinary periods of time, however an end is inevitable. We as a race have great power to slow our own entropy, but not the power to stop it. As the old saying goes, *'All good things must come to an end.'* The acceptance of this as inevitable need not be depressing, no more than the acceptance of our own mortality need be."

Noah regarded his mentor. Dr. Alec Grand had been more than a professor; he had been a friend... *almost a father*. They had shared so many hours together in and out of class debating things like this.

The features behind Grand's salt and pepper bearded face smiled at Noah with a twinkle in the china blue eyes. He went on:

"Beyond the very real possibility of a *nuclear Armageddon*; let's say we do manage to keep that *genie in the bottle,* society will eventually break down under the weight of its own size."

"...I don't understand," said Noah, not following.

"It's very simple. The evolution of man has brought him into a state where he has no natural enemies. When a species finds itself in such an environment, its population explodes out of control - *beyond its ability to support itself.* Then usually that species dies out, dragging others with it.

I remember reading about a big brouhaha in Australia where the rabbit population had escalated unchecked and began to fuck up the crops and the rest of the food chain to such a degree that people were actually in peril of starvation. The farmers began to slaughter rabbits with a vengeance with every means available, from shotguns to *electrocution*. Then the Australian equivalent to the S.P.C.A. got into it. Well, let's just say that the farmers responded to all their social conscious by doing the neighborly thing of offering them *a bowl of rabbit stew*. High ideals will always... ALWAYS take a back seat to an empty belly.

Mankind has cheated natural selection. He has no predators to thin his population, and now, people are breeding like... *rabbits*."

34

"I wouldn't say man doesn't have any predators. – *What about himself?"* asked Noah.

"Ah! Good point!" agreed Grand. "... But let's carry that a little farther. Granted - man is the most ruthless, efficient, vicious, relentless killing machine that ever sprang from the hand of God. But!...That's just it. *We've become too efficient.* Now, if we have another world war it WILL be the last one! So, now, we fall into the domain of *a no win scenario:* we can't have another all out war... *but we can't afford not to.* I hate to say it but periodic wars are essential for our survival as a species."

"What?" asked Noah, astounded by what his teacher had just suggested.

"Yes, it's true, emphasized Grand. "We need a good war every fifty years or so to keep the population in check."

"That's a gruesome attitude."

"I know, but you've got to look at the big picture. Like I was saying, we've become too efficient. Now, if we have another big war nothing in the biosphere will survive but the cockroaches, so now, all we can have is little wars, which don't kill enough people to do any good. All they do is cause misery and destruction without reaping any long term benefit. Again - man's not playing by the rules. *He's cheating natural selection."*

"I can't believe you are actually advocating war."

"Your body needs a certain amount of bacteria for digestion. If your body was completely sterile it would die. The wrong kind, or too much bacteria, and you'd get sick, a little more and you die. Now, tell me Noah, is bacteria a good or an evil thing?"

"...I guess its relative."

"Precisely."

"But that seems awfully indiscriminate."

"Yeah, but who's gonna decide who deserves to live and who deserves to die. Hitler tried that and you see what happened there. Noah, I wouldn't share this with just anyone. Use that wonderful mind of yours and try to look at the forest instead of the trees.

If there are no wars, larger and larger populations will have to compete for the same finite resources. It is an inescapable conclusion that everyone's standard of living will have to go down. When you slice the pie into more pieces, the size of the pieces has to get smaller. Remember what I said: *high ideals always take a back seat to an empty belly*. If mankind's prime motivation becomes finding enough food to survive: art, literature, and science will be abandoned, and we will fall back into a dark ages."

"No, no, I can't believe that would ever happen. I'm sure before the situation ever got that bad, people would start practicing stricter birth control," said Noah, disagreeing.

"There you go again, Noah! You keep trying to put man in control of nature, *when nature is really the one in charge.* First of all, the *Catholics* would never go along with that, and second, when push comes to shove people will never voluntarily give up their own personal freedom for the good of the collective majority... *and people are going to screw and that's all there is to that.* That's not the sort of thing you can legislate."

"Well, I'm sure when people realized the gravity of the situation they'd be willing to make use of contraceptives, and abortion laws would be repealed despite the objection of organized religion. Also the government would probably make birth control devices and abortions more readily available to the general populace," Noah pointed out.

"Wrong!" exclaimed Grand. "… At least the first part anyway. The second part, I have no doubt.

I spent eight weeks in India summer before last. While I was there I spent some time touring a hospital in Calcutta. Of course, you know the population problems they have. Anyway, the staff at the hospital told me about a program the Indian government was trying to implement, where they were giving out condoms to the general public free of charge... This sound like the scenario you just outlined?"

"Yeah."

"Guess what they did with the condoms?"

"What?"

"...Blew them up, tied the ends, and made little balloons out of them, then sold them in the marketplaces for the equivalent of a dime."

Noah was speechless.

Grand was amused. He continued: "You seem to think everyone is reasonable and intelligent. There are some incredibly stupid people in the world, Noah.... A LOT OF THEM!

While I was at the Calcutta hospital, one of the doctors there told me of one chap with eight kids whom he was trying to attempt some measure of family counseling with. The bloody fool sat there in his office saying, *'I don't know what's wrong, seems like we just have a kid every year or so. I don't know why.'*

As ridiculous as that sounds, I bet you could find some clinic doctor or social worker in this very county who could tell you a similar story.

Oh sure, there are many people who are enlightened enough to look beyond their immediate circumstance, but in this day and age, those people wouldn't have eight children anyway, and the ones that would are subsidized by the welfare state. See what I mean about one species growing unchecked brings down the others? Who finances the welfare state? - *The middle class.* And as the welfare state grows, it becomes more and more burdensome - thus the standard of living will have to go down for everyone.

The welfare segment of the population will continue to grow by leaps and bounds. So, it is obvious that the middle class will be an endangered species. The upper class is doomed also, for without the middle class, there's no one to do the work. As the middle class shrinks the resources of the welfare state will become more limited - thus everyone's poverty increases proportionately. And yet again, *high ideals will take a back seat to empty bellies.* The lower classes will become as sheep, and fall prey to drug lords, con artists and violent criminals. Their neighborhoods will become war zones, which will encroach upon the cities of the world, until one day we will wake up in the middle of a dark ages of ignorance and civil war - ***Witness the devolution of man.***"

"...Is that what you believe?" Noah said after some length, almost stunned by the barrage of doom Grand had hurled at him.

Grand looked at Noah and suddenly burst into laughter. "Yes, I suppose I do... either that or a nuclear holocaust, or maybe someday an asteroid will smash into the earth and we'll all go the way of the dinosaurs."

Noah took a long breath and said blinking, "Well, why do you even bother getting up in the morning, if you can see only doom in the future?"

Again, Grand laughed, and patting Noah on the knee said, "I didn't say that all I saw in the future was doom."

"So, what's all this shit you've been telling me?"

"All I'm really saying is that to all things in the natural universe there is an end. But so far I've only told you half of it. With all endings there are new beginnings. Civilization after civilization have bit the dust: the Romans, the Myians, the Aztecs - all gone. It is the epitome of arrogance to think that *ours* must endure forever. Like all living things we have a season. It's up to us as a people to make the best of our season. Our civilization will one day fall too, but another will take its place, and then one day it will fall, and another take its place."

"But it's all such a ... such a ... cosmic waste of time! The way you would have it each successive civilization would have to re-invent the wheel."

"It's not a waste of time. What we accomplish is not nearly as important as the struggle that is involved to meet the challenge. Noah, I'm 50 years old. I've been around the world a half a dozen times. I've gone everywhere; done everything, and I have a room full of university degrees. But even though there is still much to do in my lifetime I'd trade everything for what I see in your eyes right now. I've lost my innocence, and without innocence there can be no wonder."

"I don't get it," said Noah.

Alec Grand smiled a fatherly smile towards his student, and then continued, "...You are just starting the adventure. There are so many things ahead for you to learn, and the wonder you will feel as you learn and discover is really the only thing which makes it worth while.

It's that way with a civilization; and note that I'm not talking about size. *When something ceases to grow, it starts to die.*"

There was a long silence between them. Then Dr. Grand, in scarcely more than a whisper, asked, "Noah?"

"Yeah?"

"Do you believe in God?"

Noah thought a moment and said, "No, Dr. Grand, I really doubt that there's an old man up there on a cloud somewhere calling the shots."

"...It's a pity ... It would be so much easier if you did. There are so many things in creation you've just gotta take on faith. Everything happens for a reason - good and bad. We're just too small to understand God's grand scheme. When you're in the middle of the woods all you see is trees, so it's hard to believe in something called a *forest*.

I said nothing is permanent. That's not entirely true. Life is eternal. Oh, it changes its shape. One thing dies, and decays, and becomes fertilizer for the birth of something else."

He pointed at the sky. The view was breathtaking. Alec Grand's country home was miles from town so the visibility was clear enough to even see the Milky Way.

"All those stars will one day burn out. But then their spent matter will implode back upon itself becoming denser and denser ... iron atoms breaking down into carbon ... carbon to oxygen ... oxygen to helium ... then finally there won't be matter at all - just elemental energy. There won't even be gravity or electromagnetism or even space as we would recognize it. Time itself will cease to be. Then in the vast empty darkness of the nothingness the voice of God will thunder 'LET THERE BE LIGHT!' and it will start all over again."

The two pondered the prospect in quiet meditation. Then suddenly, a shooting star streaked across the shimmering curtain of stars. Dr. Grand finished his drink and sat the glass down on the concrete floor: ice cubes rattling softly. He took a deep breath and said, *"You've just gotta have faith."*

CHAPTER THREE

The girl rattled the ice cubes in her empty glass. "Buy me a drink?"

"Huh? ...What?" stammered Noah, startled; coming back to the present.

A young woman three seats down from him raised her glass and rattled the ice cubes again, then smiled as she repeated, "I said, buy me a drink?"

Noah looked her up and down. *Yes, this was the one.* He made eye contact with the bartender. "Hey! ... Another *Salty Dog* for the lady."

She smiled and nodded in gratitude.

She was a black woman in her early twenties, dressed in a light blue tube top and a bright orange mini-skirt. Her taut midriff was bare, and the nipples of her breasts protruded through the fabric of the garment. She wore her hair straightened; reminiscent of styles normally chosen by white women. She had a broad pleasant smile of brilliant white teeth.

The barkeep brought the drink and sat it down in front of her as Noah sat down on the bar stool next to her, carrying his own beer mug down to the last quarter of its contents. She picked up the drink and held it up in salute before taking the first sip.

"So, what's your name, big boy?" she said, smiling at the triteness of the cliché.

"Noah," came his answer.

"Like in the Bible?" she asked.

"Like in the Bible," he answered. "What's yours?" he asked, then drained the rest of his beer and motioned to the bartender for another.

"Lavonne."

"That's French, isn't it?"

"I suppose," she said, then slid her hand along the inside of Noah's thigh. "Ever party with a black girl, Noah?" Lavonne asked, getting right down to business.

Noah felt his erection swell as he answered coolly, "No, but I've heard its all pink inside."

Lavonne giggled, removed her hand, and took a sip from her drink. "Once you've had *brown sugar* you'll never go back."

"Shy, aren't you?"

"You don't get nowhere being shy."

"I bet you're real popular."

"I ain't had no complaints."

"I bet you haven't."

She fumbled in a tacky metallic silver purse for a package of cigarettes, found it, extracted one, put it in her mouth, then scratched around inside the purse again for a lighter. Noah pulled out his own lighter, obliging her to abandon the search. She leaned toward Noah for him to light the cigarette, which he did.

"So..." she began, then took a deep drag off the cigarette and exhaled violently, "...think you might wanna have a little party?"

"You make the offer sound rather tempting."

"Somehow it sounds kinda funny to tempt a man named *Noah*," she said ruefully.

"That's all right, I'm used to *animals*," Noah said as his features hardened and his *killer's eyes* peeked out for a glimmer of a moment.

Lavonne lost her smile as an alarm in the back of her head started to go off. Hookers have to develop a sixth sense about people. Judgments have to be made as to whether you're dealing with a *horny john* or a *serial killer*. And often you're faced with the question: *who's going to hurt me more, the serial killer or my pimp if I don't bring home any money.*

"I'm sorry, I didn't mean it to sound that way," Noah said, turning back on the charm.

Lavonne took another drag off her cigarette and studied the man before her. He was middle age, tall, trim and wiry. He had dark brown hair, graying at the temples. He wore a tan shirt and khaki pants. All he needed was a pith helmet and he would have looked right at home on safari. The heat of the August evening had made him perspire; leaving large sweat stains under his armpits. Still, all in all, he didn't look too bad - *for an old white man.* She had had to fuck a lot worse... *But there was something real creepy about his eyes.*

She took another sip of her drink and visibly came to a decision. *She would risk it.* "I know a place right up the street from here that's a little more uh... *private.*"

"That's all right; my hotel is just a few blocks from here."

Lavonne's warning bell was going off. She studied his face. He seemed pleasant enough - *but those eyes!* She said nothing.

"If a fella was to want to have a little party... how much is the... uh, *cover charge?*"

Damn! He's definitely a paying customer..."That all depends on how much of a party you're looking for. Fifty for a *fast lane*, a hundred for an *all niter.*"

"I don't know if I could stand an *all niter*, but I suppose I'm game for *the fast lane*. I'm celebrating. *It's my birthday.*"

"Well, happy birthday."

"Thank you."

They bantered back and forth for about fifteen minutes or so, then got up and headed for the door. Lavonne walked ahead of Noah swinging her hips in a well practiced choreography; the tight orange skirt showcasing her well rounded hind parts.

When they arrived at Noah's room, he shut the door, and they began to embrace. She stopped him and insisted on being paid up front. When he handed her the fifty, it was almost as if he had dropped a coin in a pinball machine. *She became alive.* Her kisses felt hot against his lips as she became more passionate. He made a shuttering sound as her probing tongue found its way into his ear. He ran his fingers through her hair finding it rough and coarse, not very pleasing to his touch; but groping her derriere and breasts did please him very much. Her body was soft, but firm, round and full in all the right places, and lean and flat in the others.

When she had worked him up to a good boil, she went into the bathroom and stayed for what seemed like an awfully long time. When she returned Noah had stripped to his tank-top and boxers, and was sitting at the desk smoking a cigarette. She stood before Noah holding his face in her hands. Her hands were soft, and felt cool upon his cheeks. He could smell her cheap perfume, it smelled like *air freshener*. She pulled the tube top over her head and her naked breasts jiggled as they were freed from the skin tight garment. They were not especially large, but they were wonderfully shaped and proportioned. The aureoles: dark brown; the size of half dollars. The nipples: erect and hard. Noah kissed her breasts. They were smooth, and the skin stuck to his lips a little as he methodically caressed their round symmetries. His hand ran along the curve of her waist and along her back as she ran her fingers through his close cropped hair.

He stood up and kissed her long and hard, this time his tongue slipped into her mouth as he unzipped the tight orange skirt, sending it falling down around her ankles. He was mildly surprised to find she wore no underwear. At this point she began to peel his undershirt upward. He stepped back and raised his arms over his head, helping her to unclothe his torso. The shirt was sweaty and clung to his body. She stepped out of the skirt around her ankles and kicked off her shoes. With their nude bodies entwined, they inched their way onto the bed. Noah slivered out of his boxer shorts.

After ten minutes of hurried foreplay the couple assumed the missionary position, and soon *the pictures on somebody else's wall were rattling*. Noah listened to Lavonne moan. He smiled to himself as he thought, either she was really having a good time or she was an accomplished actress. Then he came inside her and felt with great satisfaction his semen explode into her body ... *mission accomplished.*

*****

He watched the orange tip of his cigarette glow. The room was in semi-darkness, lit only by the light escaping from the bathroom. Noah listened to Lavonne's urine splash into the toilet. Presently, the toilet flushed. He got up and went into the bathroom to find the woman washing her face, her bare backside arousing him. He put his arms around her waist and began to kiss her neck, then slowly slid his hands up her chest to hold each breast cupped in his hands.

She pulled away from him smiling. "Uh huh... Now, Noah, honey, *that'll be extra."*

"But it's my birthday."

45

She was looking at him through the mirror, for she had not turned around yet as she said, "Do you have any idea how many times I've heard that line?"

Noah laughed and began to massage her shoulders. "I bet... quite a few times." Then he started to massage her neck.

Lavonne closed her eyes and swayed her head back and forth slowly. "...mmm...mmm...mmmmmmmmmm... but you can do that all night long and I won't charge you a dime."

Noah began to consider Lavonne's delicate neck. He thought to himself absently how simple it would be to snap it like a dry twig. He already had his hands around it - one quick twist - *she'd never know what hit her*. He studied the blissful features of her face reflected in the mirror. He thought to himself, *"What a fool you are... standing there with your eyes closed with that goofy look on your face. You have no idea you are a dead woman."*

His eyes traveled up and down her feminine frame, then for the first time he noticed how similar it was to *Marion's*. Maybe he noticed it on some subconscious level, and that's why he had chosen her. He marveled at the similarity. *It may have been black - but that was definitely Marion's butt!*

CHAPTER FOUR

A slightly younger Noah Little sat soaking luxuriously in a large sunken bathtub staring lustfully at Marion Grand's ass, thinking to himself that it was certainly something to behold. The room was huge and pretentious, with its marble floor and fixtures; an extension of his ex-wife's personality. She had been gone but six months when Noah replaced her with this beauty standing before him, nude, her back turned, enthusiastically flossing her teeth in the large gold trimmed bathroom mirror. Marion Grand was a tall, slender woman in her late twenties. She was quite handsome in a tomboyish sort of way. She had wild, frizzy, light brown hair half way down her back and alert hawk-like features. She was brilliant, energetic, driven, goal oriented; everything Marie had not been. She was a third year medical student who worked in Noah's lab, and as of quite recently... *shared his bed.* - She was also Alec Grand's granddaughter.

Noah got up out of the tub, dried off, and slipped on his robe. He walked over to Marion and pinched a butt cheek. She jumped with a little squeal, and then elbowed him playfully.

"You better get-a-move-on professor, if you're gonna make that eight o'clock!" she chirped.

"Yeah, I know..." groaned Little, kissing her on the back of the neck.

"Geeze Noah, why in the hell did you schedule that thing so damn early in the morning?"

"You know what they say - *the early bird gets the worm!"*

"Yeah, *but Gross Anatomy*! ...I believe there's gotta be a sadistic streak in you - to make people screw around with cadavers that close to breakfast - ooooooooh!"

Noah responded with a dastardly laugh. Then went off into the bedroom to dress.

The next fifty minutes included dressing - Noah in a tweed suit, and Marion in very tight jeans and a sweatshirt inscribed with, "I DON'T WANNA HEAR IT!" in large block letters across the front - a quick breakfast of English muffins and pop tarts, and a rather lively drive to the campus in which Marion drove and Noah watched the floorboard. She dropped him off in front of the building where he was to hold his anatomy class, and then spun away to the other side of the campus, the white convertible Mercedes screeching tires a little on takeoff.

*****

When Todd Dillow entered the laboratory Marion gave him the *evil eye*. Todd looked at her apologetically, and started to tell her why he was nearly 45 minutes late, when she placed the tips of her fingers over his mouth and shook her head. He was often late, and she was way past the point of caring to know the reasons. Then noticing the huge cardboard box he was carrying asked, "What's all this shit?"

"I dunno, but there's four more just like it at the reception desk. Some kinda of research material from Larson, Minnesota that Dr. Little had sent up here."

" ...*Humph*...he never told me to be expecting anything like that," she said furrowing her brow in distaste. "Oh, well. You better run along and get the rest of it before he gets in here or there'll be hell to pay," Marion said, then raised the sleeve of her white lab coat to examine her wristwatch. "It's almost three-thirty."

"Sure thing, Mary. I'm right on it," said Todd, turning to go. He had only made three steps when Noah came through one of the two swinging doors, narrowly missing the young man in his haste.

"Dr. Little..." gasped Todd.

"Tardy again are we, Mr. Dillow?" asked Noah; annoyed.

"I'm sorry sir. It won't happen again."

"That'll be a pleasant surprise, Mr. Dillow. Please, don't let me keep you from whatever it was that you found so urgent."

Todd left hurriedly.

Marion grinned, doing her best not to burst into laughter. "He's really not such a bad guy," she said.

"Mmm...yes," said Noah putting on his lab coat.

"A bunch of stuff came in from Larson, Minnesota."

"Where?" asked the irritated scientist looking around for the subject of their discussion.

"Over there," said Marion, pointing to the box which Todd had just brought in.

Noah donned his reading glasses: small horn rimmed half glasses he needed for close work. He examined the label, looked over his glasses at Marion and gave her a quick nod, then started for his office.

Marion followed him with her eyes as he gave her his back. "Well?" she asked.

Noah stopped walking and turned to face her. "Well, what?"

Marion smiled and nodded towards the package. "What's in the box, Doc?"

Noah started to speak then stopped. He smiled. "Well, *Pandora* ...if you must know, its research notes I made back when I was developing a hoof and mouth vaccine." Then he turned and started back for his office.

"Well... screw you, *Professor Charming*."

"Please have Mr. Dillow bring everything into my office - there should be more."

"Hoof and mouth vaccine?" queried Todd as he entered, this time with the four remaining boxes on a hand truck.

"The boss says to put all of that in his office... and be careful - somebody musta *pissed in his corn flakes today*."

"Thanks for the warning."

"...Can't understand why though - *he was in a terrific mood this morning.*"

"Hey! ...A little salt for my wounds, please."

"Now, now, be a good sport."

"I can't help it. I'm a sore loser. What ya say Mary? I'm gonna give ya one more chance at the kid."

"Thanks, but no thanks," said Mary with a mischievous smile as she sat down on a stool and activated a centrifuge.

Todd wheeled his burden up next to her and stopped. "What do you see in that old geezer anyway?"

Marion put on her own reading glasses, picked up a clipboard and scanned its contents saying, "*I love him for his mind.*"

"Hey girl, if you'd just give me half a chance I'd lay some moves on you that I'm sure would *make you change your mind.*"

Marion swiveled around on the stool and pulling her glasses down on the bridge of her nose, said in her best Noah Little impression, "*My Mr. Dillow, we certainly are full of our self this afternoon, aren't we?*"

"That's funny, Mary," said Todd, and started to wheel his way back to Noah's office, "...that's REAL funny. You oughta be on T.V."

To say that Todd Dillow had the *hots* for Marion would be a pretty fair appraisal of the situation. To say that as far as Marion Elizabeth Grand went, he was *whipping a dead horse,* would be equally fair. Todd was a tall good looking man with curly blonde hair and emerald green eyes. He was a pre-med student on a baseball scholarship. He worked hard and was an exceptional student. *He was late a lot.* It was little wonder, for he spread himself so thin he was in danger of blowing away in a strong wind. As part of a work study program, he worked in Little's laboratory taking care of the lab animals and anything else that Dr. Little had for him to do.

Marion was on a similar work study, though she hardly needed the money; her family was quite wealthy. She was there basically to learn anything she might from the illustrious *Noah Jonas Little.* Her grandfather spoke of him almost with reverence. Over her undergraduate and graduate years she became the unofficial lab manager, and did all the administrative and managerial duties, part of which had been to hire lab assistants. As Noah Little was involved in projects with varying degrees of complexity, the number of employees varied accordingly. Now, was a particularly slow period. Their only employee was Todd Dillow, as Dr. Little seemed to be between research projects waiting for inspiration. Marion had a hunch that the newly arrived boxes from Minnesota signaled the end of the lull.

When she had hired Todd Dillow she had liked him right off. Now, after two years he seemed family. She was physically attracted to him; even respected him and expected him to one day become a brilliant physician. And like everyone who came into contact with him *(even Noah, though he wouldn't admit it),* was at times susceptible to his boyish charm. Still, she always thwarted his passes.

Marion Grand hid it well, but *she was a bit of a snob.* She thought he was beneath her.

When Noah's wife divorced him, Marion saw it as an opportunity to improve her social stature and threw herself at the scientist. Marion Grand was the kind of woman who usually got what she wanted. Her family was flabbergasted, especially her grandfather. But as she was a grown woman and had proven all her life to be radically tenacious, they gradually learned to live with the fact that their daughter was living with, and probably would marry, a man almost twice her age. Although, the fact that the man in question had won the *Nobel Prize*, and was almost a legend in the field of cancer research... *knocked a little of the curse off.*

*****

When Marion entered the cage room she found Todd walking around with Chester on his shoulder, whistling: *As Time Goes By.* Chester was a small spider monkey to whom Todd had took a shine. She made it a point to not get too close to the lab animals, for they usually met with fairly hideous fates.

When Todd saw her he stopped sweeping, leaned on his broom, and said in a pretty fair Bogart, *"...Of all the zoos, animal clinics and dog pounds - she had to walk into mine."*

"Well, Todd, my man, it looks like we're back in business. Dr. Little wants you to do an inventory of all the plastic stuff and order what ever we might be low on. And tomorrow drop by Tomlinson's and pick up some mice," said Marion, and then handed Todd a handful of small official looking documents. "Here are the purchase orders.

When you've got everything filled out, just get him to sign 'em... Oh! I know for sure we're gonna need a gross of syringes."

Todd took the forms and did a curt military salute, which Chester promptly imitated.

"I've got to go to the library before it closes to look up a few things. Do you think you could stay and give Dr. Little a ride home?" Marion requested.

"Sure no problem. So... you know what we're gonna be workin' on?"

Marion sighed. "As near as I can tell... *it looks like some cow disease.*"

CHAPTER FIVE

Weeks turned into months, and Todd and Marion found out very little about the project in which they were engaged. Whatever it was; they were really wiping out white mice. The chemicals they were injecting into the little rodents were apparently pretty toxic. Each day they received lengthy reports from veterinarians. Noah kept sending Marion to the library and to the department of public health gathering statistics and any information she could find on *of all things: V.D.* Then, expensive scientific equipment began to be delivered from time to time, and packages from Minnesota vets started to come by special couriers containing live viruses.

Noah began having Todd to come in at strange hours to modify incubator environments. Then Marion would spend most of her free time behind a microscope cataloguing how the viruses from the incubators had mutated. *What in the hell were they doing?* The question hung in the air like a bad smell.

When Marion would ask Noah what was going on, at first he would say nothing. When she pressed the issue he became evasive. If she persisted he became downright hostile, and a look would come in his eyes that sent shivers up and down her spine. He would keep late hours and often would spend the night in the laboratory.

When he did come home he usually woke her up and would unceremoniously *jump her bones*, then when he was through, roll over and go to sleep. If any other man had done that to her she would have told him to go straight to hell, but she found herself strangely dominated by the mysterious professor, and part of her was somehow frightened of him.

Then came the rabbits. Noah had Todd breeding rabbits, and from the initial stock the population soon grew near a hundred. The first ones where inoculated with some sort of *secret potion* which Dr. Little would make himself from the viruses. Afterwards they would be perfectly healthy for a while, then would get sick and die, but their offspring would die before maturity as well. And all of the rabbits would always die from weird maladies. Sometimes their bones would turn into something almost like rubber. Their brains would swell and turn into some sort of gelatinous material. Their fur would fall out and sores would speckle their bodies. Todd helped Marion do an autopsy on one and to their utter astonishment found that the animal had no blood! ... *It was scary*.

*****

Noah lay in darkness staring up at the ceiling while Marion clung to him with her head resting on the left side of his chest. Her eyes; now accustomed to the shadows could make out his face, and was aware of his open eyes staring blankly upward. He had come home shortly past ten that evening and was a little more attentive than he had usually been of late. *Which really wasn't saying a whole lot*. They had just finished sex, and it had been pretty good. It was more accurate to say they had had *sex,* rather than to say that they had *made love*. Noah could be charming when he wanted to be, and he was definitely experienced, and knew all sorts of bedroom acrobatics, but the best he could do was leave Marion feeling *satisfied - never loved*.

Tonight, Marion felt profoundly lonely. She longed for a *lover, not just a sex partner*. She also knew that this situation she now found herself in was her own doing.

She had made her bed, now, she would have to lie in it... *and tonight she was finding it a particularly cold one*.

She shifted her position slightly, rested her chin on Noah's chest and played absently with his chest hair; making slow circles with her left hand. Noah moved slightly to see what she was doing, and then resumed his vigil at the ceiling.

"Penny for your thoughts, Professor," said Marion softly.

He looked at her without moving his head, and then returned his gaze back to the ceiling. He sighed.

"Marion?"

"Mmmmm?"

"Have you ever thought that some people don't deserve to live?"

"What?" she asked, raising up.

Noah rolled over and they changed positions so they could face each other.

"Have you ever thought the world would be better off without certain people?"

Marion considered for a moment, and then said, "Well, I never really thought about it, but I suppose we could have done without people like *Hitler... Joseph Mengele* ...and people like that, I guess."

"No, that's not what I meant. I mean do you think there are segments of the population living today that the world as a collective whole would be better without?

"...Like murderers and rapists?"

"Yeah, that's... that's sorta what I mean, but a little more broad based: all criminals and ...and ...and basically people who don't make a positive contribution."

Marion thought for a long time, and then said, "I'm not sure I'm following you, Noah".

Noah took a long breath. "Back when I was an intern at Christ Hospital in Los Angeles, I used to work the emergency room. I'd see it all: gang wars, child molestations, drug O.D.s, you name it. And it looked to me like they wouldn't even try to do better... It looked like they were content to be what they were - *proud of it even*."

Marion interjected, "That's not really fair. A person has to have self-respect. And also those people you are speaking of never had any of the advantages that you and I have had. They're in a situation where survival is a top priority, and as far as making positive contributions like I think you are speaking of, like say... *becoming doctors*, well, they don't have access to educational opportunities."

"Yeah, I used to think like that. But after being there I'm not so sure anymore. The people I met were only interested in shootin' heroin and boostin' someone's car."

"Noah, you know as well as I do that drug addiction can make people lose perspective on what's legal and what's not. When the human body is in that kind of substance withdrawal the only thing that matters is stopping the pain, and if breaking into someone's home and lifting a television will stop it, I'm sure that most people would risk any consequence."

"Yeah, but why don't they go out and get a fucking job!"

"Well, would you hire anyone like that?"

"...No...I suppose I wouldn't."

"Well, then..."

"But there's all kinds of drug treatment programs available. Why don't they go get their shit together?"

"Kicking a heroin habit isn't like trying to get a child to stop sucking his thumb. And as far as treatment goes... you can't just give someone a shot and go: *There, all better!"*

"That's the point I'm trying to make. There is something inherently wrong with those people. *They're weak.* Oh, not physically, most of them could and would break you in half if you gave 'em a sideways look, *but they're weak inside.* They have no self-control. If they want something and they can't buy it - *they take it.* They abuse their bodies with all the drugs because they lack the will power to abstain, and then use their addiction as an excuse. And you're not gonna tell me that they don't know better. This day and age they teach kids from kindergarten what illegal drugs can do.

And another thing; when they get horny - they fuck! - *Damn the consequences.* Far be it for 'em to take a half a second to stop off and buy a condom. So, they breed like dogs and the children grow up to be just like them."

"Yeah, but look at the kind of life they're forced to lead. Their parents abuse them; the peer pressure is tremendous to do the drugs, and their school teachers have to spend more time in the role of policemen than they do as educators."

"Please spare me the old drill about *environment versus heredity* 'cause I'm not buying it. My father grew up dirt poor, working on a dairy farm back in Minnesota, and he put himself through college, and then went on to veterinary school, and made a nice life for all of us growing up. If a person doesn't have defective genes he will adapt and thrive anywhere."

Noah was silent for a while thinking furiously. Marion began to see his point - *but didn't agree with it.* She was about to debate the issue further when suddenly Noah started to speak again.

"...And defective genes are not limited to people who live in slums. There are people who live at the pinnacle of society who are just as useless to the collective good of mankind as the most common garden variety low life gutter trash.

You take Marie. She was the weakest woman there

has ever been. Totally useless. If some of your poor under privileged delinquents had a third the opportunities afforded to her, I must concede, they probably would have amounted to something. But Marie! Now, she never worked hard at anything in her life. *Everything just fell into her lap because she had big tits!"*

"What!" Marion exclaimed.

"It's true. That woman is a millionaire today, and she didn't lift a finger for any of it. *She just aimed those 38D's in my face, and all the blood musta run right out of my brain straight into my penis."*

"Noah!"

"You women have always had the advantage over men when it comes to things like that. *All a woman really needs to be successful in life are big tits and a round ass!"*

Marion sat up in the bed mad as a hornet. "Noah Jonas Little! I never knew you were such a chauvinist son of a bitch!" she said, exasperated.

"The truth hurts, don't it, toots?"

She got up and stood beside the bed. "From now *on you can beat your meat*, Dr. Little!

Noah sat up in the bed. "You see that proves my point exactly. It must be part of the DNA code of all women. See, I've won this debate with irrefutable logic, and now that you see that you don't stand a chance in a fair fight, by instinct, you're using your body as a sexual weapon. You think by withholding sexual favors you can exercise some control over me. Well, think again, bitch! I could have another one just like you tomorrow. All you are is a piece of meat. Besides, you think I don't know why you're here. You think I can help your career. Well, I can. I can open doors for you that you never even imagined, as long as you continue to be a good fuck. But you better lay off that pie, baby, because if your ass gets much bigger you're hittin' the bricks. That's all you are to me anyway so you better take care of your assets."

Marion burst into tears and fled the room like it was on fire. Noah watched her leave, and after a moment, fell back onto his pillow, exhaled loudly, and said, "... Shit!"

*****

The next morning was Saturday, and found the three of them: Noah, Marion, and Todd Dillow at the laboratory busy putting in yet more time on *the great secret project*. As the morning turned into afternoon, Noah left without saying farewell or stating his destination, leaving Todd and Marion to share about ten minutes of awkward silence. Todd noticed the coolness between Marion and Noah, and would have thoroughly enjoyed it if he had felt a little better; as he was in the third day of a pretty nasty cold. *As it was, he was just amused.*

Todd walked into the cage room and reached into a brown paper bag to retrieve another glazed doughnut: his *fifth... Feed a cold, starve a fever.* Marion entered moments behind him, seeming rather despondent and needing to talk to someone, *but said nothing.* Todd waited for her to begin, and when she didn't, he chattered on about this and that while her responses were at a minimum. She wouldn't spill it, but yet it was clear that she wanted to, for she just kept hanging around.

Todd looked around uncomfortably, and looking at the way the rabbit cages were arranged, was hit with a sudden revelation.

"I don't know what kind of mystery disease *Dr. Strangelove* is working on, but I believe I know how it's transmitted," Todd said as he finished his doughnut.

"How?" asked Marion, her eyes widening.

"Sexually."

60

"Huh?"

"Look at the way he's got me arranging these animals," said Todd, walking toward the rabbits with Marion following close behind. He looked at her and explained, "The first group he infected with *Professor Little's Marvelous Mystery Disease and Indian Elixir*, and then for some unknown reason the offspring start to die. Oh, the parents eventually die also but it puzzled me why the offspring died as well. See this cage?" he pointed to a cage with six rabbits inside. "Two of them have the bug, the rest of them don't. It's been six weeks the other four are perfectly healthy. They all sleep together in the same cage; they eat the same food, outta of the same dish."

Todd sneezed. "Excuse me." He led Marion to another cage. "Here you've got five infected rabbits - one perfectly healthy. So, ya see, it can't be airborne. Over there..." He pointed to a large cage with many rabbits and they walked over to it. "...Started out with twelve healthy rabbits and one infected one – *now, all of them have got it*."

"So, what's the connection?"

Todd pointed to the first cage. "...All girls." He pointed to the second; "All boys", then to the last one: "*CO-ED!*"

Marion looked from cage to cage, then backed to Todd and slowly smiled. "By George, I believe the man has actually figured it out."

Todd smiled and nodded triumphantly, then offered the open brown bag to Marion and said, "Doughnut?"

Marion reached for the bag, and then suddenly stopped just short of putting her hand inside as the smile disappeared from her face. "No thanks... *I'm on a diet*."

CHAPTER SIX

It was Monday afternoon when Noah crossed the finely groomed lawns of the campus headed for the administration building. He was apprehensive; antsy.

He went inside and murmured vague responses to all who greeted him, as he made his way through the labyrinth of offices on his way to his destination. Dean Anderson's secretary, Marge, smiled wanly and invited him to have a seat in the outer office.

He sat down, unaware how nervous he looked, flipping through the pages of a copy of *Psychology Today,* he had picked up off the coffee table. He wasn't really reading the magazine, just holding it, while he turned over in his mind all the possible lines of defense he could offer at the meeting he was about to walk into. He realized that his palms were sweating. There was no doubt about it - *he was scared shitless.*

"Dr. Little? They're ready for you now," Marge said cordially.

This was it. Noah rose and headed for the huge oak door that lay between him and possible ruin. Once inside he found things worse than he had feared. There were about a half of dozen men in dark, finely tailored suits; some standing, others lounging in the large overstuffed chairs of Dean Milton P. Anderson's palatial office. The group represented the bulk of the endowment trustees.

"Noah... come in, come in," invited Anderson, rising and walking around his massive desk to shake hands.

He smiled, but not sincerely. They shook hands and Dean Anderson put his hand on Noah's back, turning him toward the assembled group who seemed to scrutinize Little with an ineffable air of suspicion. "I believe you know everyone..."

Noah nodded. "Gentlemen."

The men mumbled their greetings, and Anderson motioned Noah to a large chair in front of his desk.

"Would you like a cup of tea?" Anderson asked.

"No, thank you, I'm fine," replied Noah.

Anderson leaned against the desk; his smile painted on. "...Things moving along well at your laboratory?"

"Yes, sir... very well."

"Good, good... Well, that's why we've called you to this little informal get-together. I hear through the grapevine that your Leukemia research has taken a... well ah ...taken a sort of new direction. We're always very interested in your research projects and were wondering if you might bring us up to speed on what you've been working on?"

CHAPTER SEVEN

"...You can charge the rest of that to our account," Marion informed.

The delivery man from *Allied Scientific* looked nervous. "I'm sorry, ma'am...I can't do that."

Marion frowned. "Why not?"

"...Well...fact of the matter ma'am is... *your account is three months delinquent.*"

"What?!"

"Yes, ma'am, and I was given specific instructions not to afford you anymore credit till the balance was made current."

Marion took off her glasses and put them inside the pocket of her lab coat, then said with increasing frustration, "This is impossible - there must be some sort of mistake. I've sent a half a dozen checks to *Allied* this month alone."

"Yes, ma'am, you did... *and they are all still bouncing.*"

Marion sighed. "I can't believe this. How much are we in the red?"

The man looked at the clipboard he was carrying and read off the requested figures, "Nine thousand, four hundred and seventeen dollars and twenty seven cents."

Marion just stared at the man.

"Of course, that doesn't include what I have for you today."

Marion's gaze remained fixed on the man's face for an uncomfortable length of time, then at last she asked in a quiet, but stern voice, "How much for today's delivery?"

The man consulted his clipboard again; "Seventy three dollars and forty nine cents."

Marion looked down at the floor a moment, then suddenly walked across the room, opened the door on a lab table and withdrew her purse. She then rambled through it producing the exact amount, even down to the four pennies.

She paid the man, and then he dumped off three white cardboard boxes, collected his hand truck and left. The whole of this transaction was conducted without words from either party.

Todd burst through the door with his usual jovial perkiness. "Hello, Mary," he trumpeted, then donned his white lab coat.

"Hi, Todd," Marion greeted sadly. She was upset and worried about what had just transpired a few moments ago, but it was what she had to do now, she dreaded.

Dillow noticed the boxes piled in the middle of the floor and said with mock disgust, "Oh great! Just what I've always wanted - MORE BOXES!" then started to open the top one.

"Todd?"

"Yeah."

"Before you get into that we've got another autopsy."

Todd assumed a hunchback stance and walked over to the stool where Marion sat before her microscope, dragging one foot and speaking like *Peter Lori*. "Yes, master. Yes, master. Igor will go get the instruments."

Marion gently took his arm and with pain in her eyes said, "Todd."

Todd looked at Marion's expression and his smile softened a little.

Marion looked as if she had something important to say but couldn't find tactful enough words. Finally, she opted for the direct approach. *"It's Chester."*

The rest of Todd's smile slowly faded away.

Marion watched waves of regret pass across his face. "I'm sorry, Todd."

"...It's all right - *occupational hazard.*"

"I can do it if you'd like."

"...No ...I'll help."

"You sure?"

"Yeah, I'm okay. You set up the autopsy tray and I'll... I'll go get him."

*****

The two medical students worked in silence performing their ghoulish task. Organs were removed, blood samples were taken, and tissue samples were made. Chester's skull was opened and his brain extracted. When the animal was reduced to basically a collection of jars, they peered into microscopes and pored over data to a little past eight that evening. They didn't break for dinner. *Neither had much appetite.*

Marion sat more erect, pushed her glasses back on top of her head, and passed her hands over her face, rubbing her weary eyes. "As near as I can tell this animal died of a *cold.*"

Todd was sitting with his back to her at a lab table parallel to hers on a high stool with piles of papers spread out before him in a haphazard array. He swiveled around to face her. "What did you say?"

"I said... as near as I can tell *he died of a cold.*"

"How can anything die of a *cold?*"

"Well, you've looked over all this shit the same as me, what do you think he died of?"

Todd was thoughtful for a moment. "Yeah... BUT! Same question: *how can anything die of a cold?"*

"That's the sixty four thousand dollar question, isn't it?" Marion sighed and looked down at the floor. Both stared at the same spot for a long time, then Marion sat back on her stool and swiveled back and forth as she spoke. "I've got a theory."

"Spill it, girl. I'm all ears."

"Well, you know how tight lipped Dr. Little is?"

Dillow nodded.

"From what I've seen and what little I've managed to pry outta the good doctor, looks like to me what we've been developing here is some sort of... *designer virus* that infects its host on a cellular level where it can remain dormant for a long time. But when that bad boy wakes up. Look out! It does something to the animal which disables its immune system --"

"So, any type of virus or bacteria that enters an infected host runs rampant because the animal can't manufacture any antibodies," Todd interjected as the light of comprehension began to dawn.

"Give that man a cigar! That's what all those *Twilight Zone* symptoms have been about in our lab animals. And that's what happens to living bodies when common everyday germs have their way with no resistance from an immune system," Marion explained further.

Todd whistled. "Holy Shit!"

"You damn straight, partner. Anyway... you know all that crap we kept getting from all those veterinarians?"

"Yeah."

"Back about ten or fifteen years ago Noah was workin' with a bunch of vets in Minnesota. They were all goin' ape shit over this strain of hoof and mouth disease that would mutate every time someone would try to treat it - *highly adaptable.* Well, our golden boy saved the day with this breakthrough vaccine that would kill the sucker.

Those live viruses we've been getting in are from that same strain, and we've been mutating them into the *Virus from Hell."*

Todd stood up and began to pace a little. "Mary, we're dealing with some serious shit here."

"Tell me about it."

"That virus is as tenacious as a mother fucker. You couldn't kill it with a M-16! *What if that thing got loose and infected a human host?"*

A chill ran through the core of her very soul. She looked wide-eyed at Todd and spoke in controlled even tones.

"It would probably remain dormant for five or six years, then the same thing that happened to those animals would happen to..."

Todd looked gravely at Marion and asked, *"And what if the infected person had an active sex life?"*

"Oh, my God! Every person who had relations with the infected host would..."

"...Would have the disease. And that person would pass it on to whoever they had sex with, and that person would pass it on, and on and on..." Todd finished.

A sick feeling seized the pit of Marion's stomach. Todd sat back down and they both looked at each other in horror.

"It'd make the black plague look like diaper rash," Marion said at last.

"Well, one thing's for sure. I bet it'd put a hellva damper on *the sexual revolution,*" Todd remarked.

"Todd, we don't have the facilities here to be working with something this dangerous."

"Do you think Dr. Little is working for the government?"

"...No ...Why?"

"Well, all of this sounds like some sort of germ warfare to me. Maybe they're planning to drop this shit on the Russians."

Marion considered the possibility, and then rejected it. "No, Todd, I'm absolutely sure we're not working for the government."

"How can you be so sure?"

"Because if we were working for the government we would be better funded. Something weird happen just before you got here today. This man from *Allied Scientific* came in and told me our account was over nine thousand dollars in the red."

"Nine thousand dollars?"

"He said all the checks I've sent to them for the past three months have bounced."

"Whew!" he exclaimed, and then Todd Dillow ..... *sneezed.*

"Bless you."

"Thanks," he said, then took out his handkerchief and applied it to his nose.

"Haven't you got rid of that cold yet?" asked Marion.

Suddenly, they both looked at each other astonished.

"He got it from me, didn't he?"

CHAPTER EIGHT

Marion Grand hadn't noticed the traffic light had changed till she was startled by the blaring horn of the car behind her. She shifted her red Porsche 924 into gear and started down the street. Her mind raced over the implications of what had happen today. *What did it all mean: a killer virus, dead animals, germ warfare, the lab's failed bank account?* **And what connection could the project have with all that creepy research she had done last fall on venereal diseases?**

She began to recall fragments of data on how various forms of V.D. spread, and just how prevalent it really was. *What if their bug got out and spread via the same apparatus and on the same magnitude...?* One thing was for certain, a shot of penicillin wouldn't kill it. Todd was right; *to say the virus was* **hardy** *would be like calling the Queen Mary: a fairly nice boat.* To hell with atomic bombs - it might take a hundred years or so but their virus had the potential of wiping out the entire human race just as completely.

Marion flashed on pictures she had seen of the great ancient cities in South and Central America: great civilizations whose inhabitants had just vanished without a trace. *Would that be the fate of the human race? Would everyone die off leaving all the cities to be swallowed by the forests and the jungles? Mankind's big finish:* **a whimper; not a bang.**

She realized in horror the notion wasn't so farfetched. One thing she had learned from studying venereal diseases was that the compulsion to have sex seemed to be far greater than the fear of contracting a disease. In modern times maybe people weren't nearly as frightened of such things because generally, *there was a cure.* However, in Victorian Europe it had been fairly common for people to die of syphilis, and that threat didn't seem to slow things down one bit. Their virus would be a return to those times, *only worse.* Once Dr. Little's virus inhabited a host, it was *100% incurable.* And coupled with the fiendish aspect of the infected person not even knowing he or she had the disease for 5 to 7 years, could allow the scourge to infect hundreds of thousands of people before the medical community would have an inkling of what they were dealing with. *Hell - she knew what to look for, and a lot of times she failed to diagnose it in some of their laboratory animals till their brains had turned into marmalade!* Then add all of that to how long it would take for people to become educated to the danger; and to the bitter end there would always be people thinking, *"It couldn't happen to me."*

Marion thought of how careless they had been with the viral cultures. Work like that should be carried out in a sealed, airtight laboratory, under the strictest security and contamination protocols. Now, it seemed ludicrous. *It was like building a hydrogen bomb in your basement.*

*****

She turned into the long winding driveway leading to Noah Little's mansion. When she parked in front of the sprawling building she noticed Noah's white Mercedes. *She was going to have a long talk with this man.*

When she opened the front door she was greeted with the melodious chords of *Pachelbel's Canon in D*, floating softly from the den. She hung her purse on a brass coat tree, and then headed toward the music.

She found Noah in his large easy chair: head tilted back, eyes closed, holding a half a tumbler of scotch in his right hand which rested on the huge arm of the chair. He looked asleep. Then as if he heard Marion make some barely audible disturbance, opened his eyes and looked at her. She could tell - *he had had a few.*

Marion sat down in a similar chair across from him. "Noah, the time has come for us to have a serious talk about your research project," she said resolutely.

Noah stared at her coldly, then took a sip from his scotch, leaned his head back, closed his eyes, and in a distant voice said, "...No, Marion, this is not the time."

"...*Allied Scientific* canceled our credit line today..."

Noah was motionless.

"They said our checks have been bouncing."

There was still no response from the resting form.

"Well... I thought you would wanna know."

"Ah huh," he grunted vaguely.

Marion exhaled in frustration. "Chester died today."

"...Who is Chester?"

"...One of the spider monkeys."

"Ah huh."

"...We did an autopsy."

"Ah huh."

"Would you like to know the results?"

"Ah huh."

Marion was beginning to get angry, and it was starting to show in her voice. *"He died of a cold."*

Noah said nothing.

"...Did you hear me?"

"Ah huh."

"...I said he died of a ***COLD!***"

"...Probably contracted it from exposure to Mr. Dillow," Noah said distractedly.

Now, she was mad. "Noah! Don't you think that is a little fucking weird?"

"Shush! Marion, you are becoming entirely too loud."

"Oh, I'm sorry, Noah," Marion said in a musical sarcastic whine, but very softly, "...Don't you think that is a little fucking weird?"

"No, Marion," said Noah showing a little irritation now,"...It is not weird. It was anticipated, and is exactly the result I had expected when I noticed Mr. Dillow had a cold."

"Noah, we are dealing with something which could become dreadfully dangerous. I have a right to know what is going on."

Noah remained still as a statue with his eyes closed. "You have always known that my employees work for me on a need-to-know basis only. I am not in any way obligated to explain myself to you, or anyone for that matter; the course of my research work... *Miss Grand.*"

"Well, excuse me, **DOCTOR** *Little!* I was under the impression that *I was a little more than your employee.*"

Noah opened his eyes and stared at Marion with icy malice. "This seems strange to me that you would have made any such assumption, for I thought I have always made it abundantly clear that you are, and have been from the beginning, employed as my lab manager... *and my whore.*"

Marion's mouth flew opened, then quickly clamped shut: her jaw clenched, and her eyes narrowed. *She had had enough.* She stood up and marched out of the room like a woman with a mission. She went upstairs and started to pack a suitcase. She would send for the bulk of her possessions later. *Now, the only thing that mattered was getting the hell out.*

As she slammed clothing into the open case laying atop the large king size bed, she heard Noah's soft footsteps coming up the staircase. He wobbled slightly from his intoxication. Marion made no discernible acknowledgement of his arrival - *just kept packing.* Noah leaned against the doorway and watched dispassionately.

"What are you doing?" he finally asked.

"I would think that would seem fairly obvious," Marion said frostily.

Noah watched for a while longer then said," If you mean this to imply that you are leaving me; I think not".

Marion paused a moment. "You said I was an *employee...* Well, *I quit.*"

"No, I think you will not."

"Watch..."

"I'm not through with you yet."

"Tough shit."

"I don't think you are aware of exactly with whom you are dealing with here. You will leave when I say you can leave."

Marion stopped packing and looked him straight in the eye. "Fuck you, Noah Little!"

"Yes, that is exactly what you are going to do. And you are going to do it whenever I say, and in any way I fancy."

Marion stared at him in disbelief. "...You have lost your mind," she said incredulously, slammed the suitcase closed, picked it up, and headed for the door. "Have a nice life, Noah. Good bye."

She started to push past him when his arm abruptly shot out in front of her to the other side of the door frame. Their eyes locked. *He looked at her with his killer's eyes.*

Fear suddenly shot through her, and her chest became heavy with undefined terror.

"You think they'll let you graduate when they've found out you've embezzled Nine thousand four hundred and seventeen dollars?"

She retreated several steps, dropped the suitcase and put her hands on her hips. "Noah, that's a lie!"

"*Humph;* truth. Often it's not an absolute concept, but rather... the interpretation of those in power."

He removed his hand from the door facing and switched the scotch into it. He took a sip and continued:

"...And justice? *There is no justice.* There was no justice for my little daughter. Her life...just, just snuffed out...by some shit kickin' redneck drivin' around in his pickup truck. If the bastard would of kept his eyes on the road instead of guzzlin' beer and tryin' to feel up some bar slut while he was drivin' down the wrong side of the fucking highway at sixty miles an hour - *she'd be alive today.*

You think they put the son of a bitch in the gas chamber? Noooooo! ...*They took his driver's license away!*

Humph! Took his driver's license away. He can't drive! But he can breed with all the *Daisy Maes in hell and half a Georgia* till the whole world looks like fucking *Deliverance."*

"Noah, you can't blackmail me like this," Marion said, not understanding, nor caring what Noah had been saying.

"*Blackmail, blackmail* ...that's such a vulgar term...I'd prefer to call it *extortion.* But call it what you like; I most certainly can. After all, *you* write all the checks."

"You'd never make it stick. No one would believe that I'd do such a thing. I don't need it! *I have money*...I've got that much in my checking account alone.

"...People will believe anything you want them to - provided you use the right pitch. Whether you could prove your guilt or innocence would be irrelevant. Imagine the headlines: *Beautiful Millionaire Medical Student Is Really Kleptomaniac...Would Be Doctor Writes Prescription for Embezzlement...* If that kind of press got out I don't think you would have to worry about becoming *valedictorian*.

Yeah, I'd say that would be just about it for your medical career. And you can never tell; you might become such an embarrassment to the noble name of *Grand,* they might even put you out on the street without a dime. 'Course you could probably get a job as a waitress somewhere. Marie was a waitress when I met her and look at her today. *She is a millionaire who ought to be a waitress, and you would be a waitress who ought to be a millionaire.* I rather like that: two great injustices might cancel each other out. What do you think, mmm?

Too bad about poor *Granddaddy Alec* though...I imagine he would be terribly *disappointed."*

Marion slapped Noah hard across the face, knocking the drink from his hand.

At first Noah stared at her stupidly, thoroughly shocked by what she had done. To him it had been incomprehensible. Then he saw it as an insult, and hellish rage consumed him. He balled up his fist and struck Marion, sending her flying across the room. He had struck her so hard that she almost lost consciousness. He stormed over to her and pulled her to her feet.

"How dare you strike me?! If you ever do that again *I'll kill you.* Do you hear me?" He seized her by the shoulders and shook her violently." I said **DO YOU HEAR ME?!!"**

"Yes," Marion gasped between sobs.

As an after thought he slapped her, sending her reeling to the bed.

He stared at her with murderous fury in his eyes, but suddenly spoke with icy calm in his voice:

"Marion, I have had quite enough of this rebellious attitude you have been exhibiting lately.

From now on you are going to show me proper respect. Is that understood?

Marion lay on the bed weeping softly, staring up into his cynical eyes. She nodded.

"Some people were born to do great things which shape the destiny of the human race. *I am such a person.*

Some people were born to serve people such as I. *YOU, are such a person.* Do you understand that?"

Marion didn't respond.

"Do you understand?" Noah asked with the harshness suddenly back into his voice.

"Yes!" Marion blurted out in terror, and then continued to sob quietly.

"Very good," he said with the former dispassionate calm returning. "As a man I have certain needs and part of your responsibility is to satisfy those needs. And you should take it as an honor to be the one I have chosen. Think of it as having a small part in aiding a grander purpose larger than your own life.

And from now on you will do exactly as I say. *Do you understand that?"*

Again Marion nodded.

"Now; that's a good girl. And we won't have to have another one of these distasteful little altercations, will we?"

She shook her head "no."

Noah looked at her for a long time then said, "Stand up."

Marion lay on the bed, paralyzed with fear.

"Now, Marion, you're already going back on our agreement. *Simon says*,' stand up'."

Marion stood up next to the bed.

"Strip!" ordered Noah with terrible authority.

A weeping Marion Grand unbuttoned her blouse, and then took off her jeans.

Noah eyed her up and down, but with the passion of a laboratory experiment. "Now, the bra..."

Marion did what she was told, then covered her naked breasts with her hands. She had stood nude before him many times, but now, she felt as embarrassed and afraid *as if she were standing in a room full of rapists.*

Showing some irritation Noah removed her hands from her breasts. He stared at their lovely contours, and then savagely grabbed the right one, making Marion give a little squeak of pain. Then he let go and stood back a step and admired her body for a moment.

"Not very big are they? ...I'll say one thing for Marie, she might have had shit for brains but she did have a good set of tits."

He looked at her breasts long and hard then straight in Marion's tear filled eyes.

"Perhaps I was too hasty when I took you for *my whore*... Here you are standing there stark naked and *I can't even get it up*."

He looked her up and down again, then back into her eyes for what seemed to Marion an eternity. He shook his head in disappointment, then turned and left.

CHAPTER NINE

The next morning found Noah and Marion having breakfast at the small table in the kitchen, which had been their custom from happier times. Noah had his usual: two English muffins with jelly, and a cup of black instant coffee. Marion didn't have anything but coffee. She was wearing a periwinkle terrycloth robe, and her hair was disheveled. Neither said anything about what had happen the night before. Noah read his newspaper. Marion stared into her coffee cup. The scene looked much like the way things normally looked on a Tuesday morning, except for ...*Marion's black eye*.

Noah finished reading his paper, folded it neatly, and downed the last remaining swallows from his coffee mug, then looked at Marion and said, "You should stay at home today. I don't want anyone from school seeing you till the discoloration and swelling goes away. Fortunately for you, we're only a couple of days from spring break. I'll tell all concerned you have a bad flu. It shouldn't cause you to fall behind. Of course, now, I'll have to do your share of the lab work, so, don't expect me home till late this evening. You are not to leave this house for any reason as long as you are looking like that?"

The last part of what he had said was phrased as a question. She nodded appropriately.

When Noah left she remained at the table and listened to the house filling up with silence. An hour and a half after he had left, Norma Jean, the housekeeper arrived. Noah didn't like servants puttering around in his presence, so, they were instructed to do their chores while he was at school.

When Norma Jean entered the kitchen to load the dishwasher she was surprised to find Marion there. When she greeted her mistress, the smile vanished from her face as she observed the swollen black eye. *"Oh, no, it's*

happening again," she thought. She had seen this before...
many times. She went wordlessly to the refrigerator and
extracted ice, then filled the ice pack she had retrieved
from the pantry. She felt a hideous feeling of déjà when
she gave the cold compress to a grateful Marion Grand.
She had played this scene so many times before with
Marie Little. She had hoped that Professor Little's spunky
young concubine would be too gutsy to stand for such
treatment ...*apparently not.*

*****

Noah Little faced a dilemma. His funding had been
cut off. Even dancing with his fanciest footwork, he
couldn't convince the endowment trustees the merit of
continuing his grant. He had tried to disguise his current
project as *Leukemia Research.* It just wouldn't fly; the
experiments he was doing were just too far off in left field.
But he could never tell anyone the true nature of what he
was working on. *They would never understand,* and would
in all likelihood fire him from his post as a raving lunatic.

It was so frustrating; he was almost there. Just a little
more time and he would be able to implement what he had
become convinced had been his divine destiny.

No! He would not be stopped. He wrote his own
personal check for the outstanding balance to *Allied,* and
checks to several other companies he was in arrears with.
He would finance the project to the end of the term with
his own money. In the meantime, he would begin the
search for new sponsorship. It shouldn't be too difficult.
Dr. Noah Little was a man in demand. He would find
another university in which to set up shop. *He would
succeed.*

*****

Marion woke with a jolt as the sound of the doorbell chimed through the house. She was lying on a loveseat in the den. *How long had she been asleep*? She did not know. Last night's terror had not allowed her any sleep at all, so she must have fallen asleep in the den from shear exhaustion.

When she rose she found her neck stiff; probably from the position she had contorted her body while slumbering on the short sofa. She walked through the house headed for the door, her mind almost numb. She opened it. It was Todd Dillow.

Todd took one look at Marion's left eye and shock literally froze him in his tracks. He had learned from Dr. Little that Marion had not come into work that day because of a bad case of the flu, and had decided to visit her when he had finished his duties. He had felt maybe he had been responsible for her illness, like he had been for Chester's, and felt a little guilty. He thought visiting would cheer her up, and would somewhat ease his conscience. What he saw before him was an utter surprise.

"What happened to you?" he asked.

Marion looked at him strangely, and then said, "Come inside."

She led her visitor into the living room where they sat uncomfortably for a few moments. Marion put on a mask and smiled a little as she said, "Oh, clumsy me... I was running around this morning like a chicken with my head cut off and ran into the closet door. I'm all right... really. It looks a lot worse than it actually is. I thought it was kind of embarrassing, so, I just decided to stay home today... Ya know how people are. Everybody would be asking what happened and I'd have to tell this same stupid story over and over again. Hey, I just didn't feel like dealing with all that crap."

Todd looked at her dubiously. "Dr. Little said *you had the flu.*"

Marion had forgotten the cover story. She tried to recover; she sniffed, and continued the charade. "Oh, Noah worries about me too much. I've got a little cold is all. I suppose he knew how embarrassed I was and thought he'd make up something to tell everyone why I was gone. That's kinda sweet, don't you think?" *Then she gave him the fakest smile Todd had ever seen. He wasn't buying the bullshit.*

Todd looked at her with disbelief showing in his eyes, and then at length announced, "*He* did this to you."

Marion's smile shattered like a glass bottle hit with a hammer. She couldn't hold it back any longer; she burst into silent tears, then buried her face into Todd's chest.

Todd held her in his arms and made soft comforting sounds. *She felt so good.* He began to think how ironic it was. He had met so many women in his lifetime whom he had comforted this way. Women to whom he would have given anything he had. Women he would have loved. Women he would have even married. But these women rarely thought of Todd Dillow in a romantic sort of way. He was always the *big brother* they came to when their boyfriends had hurt them. He began to marvel to himself, *"Seems like the only men women fall for are the ones that treat them like shit."* He would never understand.

When she had cried it all out, she laid her head on his shoulder, and he softly stroked her long brown hair till she stopped trembling.

"Come on. Let's go get your things." said Todd.

Marion rose up and looked at him with fear in her

eyes. "No... no, Todd, it's not like that. Really. *It was my fault.*"

"Yeah, right," Todd responded with sarcasm. "I didn't see him runnin' around this morning with a shiner. As soon as I get you outta here I'm going back over there and kick his mother fuckin' ass."

"No! No, Todd, you can't do that," Marion exclaimed pulling away from him.

"I'll be damned if I can't. Who the hell does he think he is? He can't go around beatin' up women. Let's see how he gets on with somebody his own size."

"Now, Todd, I don't want you gettin' into this. You don't know him. If you get him riled he could destroy any chance you have at ever becoming a doctor. You've come too far and worked too hard to mess up your life on count of me. I'd never forgive myself. And like I said, *it was my fault.* He had been drinking, and I started an argument with him, and things got out of hand and I slapped him, then he hit me, purely out of reflex."

"Mary, that's bullshit and you know it," Todd said with anger creeping into his voice.

"Todd, I appreciate your concern; I really do, but you're reading this all wrong. Don't blow it all outta proportion and get yourself in trouble. I can handle it. I know I got a little emotional just now, but I don't need you charging to the rescue on your white horse. You really need to stay outta this, Todd. *I mean it!*"

"Dammit, Mary! He must have you *brainwashed* or something. I can't believe you're gonna take that shit off him. What kind of man would do something like that to you? - Not much if you ask me."

"Todd, I think you better go."

"What?"

"...I think you better go."

"I don't believe this! He beats the shit outta you and you're gettin' mad at me."

"I'm not mad at you... *yet.* You don't know all the facts, and now, you're jumping to conclusions. And Todd... to be completely frank, *it's none of your business."*

"Fine. Let the son of a bitch slap you silly!" Todd exclaimed in frustration as he bolted to his feet.

"...But promise me this...if this ever happens again --"

"It won't," Marion firmly interrupted, "Now, I'm serious; you better go."

Their eyes locked. Then, Todd left without farewell. When Marion heard the door slam she burst into tears again. *She had burnt all her bridges...**she was on her own now.***

CHAPTER TEN

The months that passed till the end of the term moved slowly. Noah courted one university after another in search of a new home for his project. Finally, he settled on the *Cambridge School of Internal Medicine*. Negotiations were quickly made and agreements were worked out. Marion didn't like the idea of transferring to another school for her senior year, but Noah insisted; pointing out that it would look good on her resume to have graduated from such a prestigious university. Todd was beside himself at the prospect of her going off to England with Noah Little, but realized there was absolutely nothing he could do about it. *He was also extremely concerned at the way Marion was changing.*

Marion Grand had made a startling metamorphosis from the cocky, self-assured spitfire Todd had met two years ago. Now, she carried herself with the manners of a *Mennonite school girl*. She rarely spoke outside of the routine of what she had to in her class or lab work. She was as always, brilliant in her studies and work, but now, it seemed *she had become a machine.* Todd watched helplessly as her personality slowly drained away.

At home Marion had basically become a robot. Noah said do this and she did this. He said do that and she did that. He'd snap his fingers and she would disrobe and lie down, and would remain motionless while he raped her night after night. She became more and more withdrawn and lost weight. Her eyes lost their luster and her face became ashen.

Todd Dillow on several occasions tried to work up the nerve to confront Noah, but always lost it when he looked into the man's eyes. *There was something evil there; something frightening.* Todd knew Marion had been right. If he got on Professor Little's wrong side he would destroy his career before it even got started. Noah Little radiated this ineffable aura of superiority and authority. He was a genius, and a remarkable debater. If you got into an argument with Dr. Little - *you would lose.*

About a month before final exams, Dr. Little suspended work on his research project, and two weeks were devoted to preparing the operation for its transfer to England. Files were packed in scores of boxes, viral cultures were put in special incubators designed to keep them alive for indefinite periods, and the infected animals were put to death and cremated. Then everything that was not the property of the university was sent on ahead to Cambridge where Noah and Marion would meet it as soon as they had fulfilled all their academic obligations. Todd Dillow's services were no longer needed. His employment was terminated.

*****

Three days before Noah and Marion were supposed to leave for England; Todd spotted Marion Grand walking solemnly across the campus. *She looked so sad.* He called to her.

"Mary!" he shouted.

Marion looked around for the caller. When she saw who it was she smiled broadly. Todd jogged up to her. When he hugged her he became worried, as he felt her ribs sticking out. *She was too thin; her countenance was sickly.* The two walked along the sidewalks of the park-like university campus. The grounds were lovely: all green and alive with the smell of growing things.

"Mary, are you all right?" asked Todd gravely.

Marion didn't speak at first, then smiled wanly, and said in a voice that somehow sounded as underweight as her body, "I'm fine, Todd, just fine."

"Mary... you look awful."

"Thanks a lot."

"No, I didn't mean it that way. You're getting too thin."

"Naw, I just wanna look good in my swimsuit. Besides, I know you; *you like your women with meat on their bones.*"

His expression was intense with concern. She smiled again. "We haven't talked since we shut down the lab. Have you decided what you're going to do this summer?"

He just looked at her.

"Well?"

"...I suppose I'll go to work for the *Lions Club Outreach* like I did last year," he began reluctantly. "...They run a summer camp for blind kids up in the mountains".

"That sounds rewarding."

"It is... I've done it every summer for the past three years... You still going to England?"

"Yeah."

"Mary, are you sure I can't talk you outta this. Maybe you could go with me to the mountain camp."

"Todd, we've been all over this before. It's sweet of you to offer, but... it's quite an opportunity to graduate from *The Cambridge School of Internal Medicine.*"

Todd stopped walking abruptly. "Are you transferring to *Cambridge?*"

"...Yes."

"I thought you were just going there for the summer to help him set up the new laboratory."

"No, I've decided to transfer," answered Marion, beginning to stroll again.

"Why? You're going into your senior year," asked Todd matching her slow stride.

"Think how it would look on the old resume - impressive, huh?"

"Mary, I've got a bad feeling about this."

"Damn, Todd! You're worse than my mother."

"Yeah! That's a good one. How does you're family feel about all of this?"

Marion looked at the sidewalk and said nothing.

"...I thought so. They're not too thrilled about it, are they?"

"I'm a grown woman and I make my own decisions."

"No, Mary, you don't make your own decisions. *Noah Little makes your decisions.*"

"That's not true," she said defensively.

"Isn't it?"

Marion was silent.

"He says jump and you say how high, *and would you like a back flip with it, sir?*"

Marion again made no reply.

"What kind of hold does he have on you?"

Just then a car horn blew. They turned and saw Noah's white Mercedes in the student parking lot. Marion looked at the car and then back to Todd with profound sadness showing on her face.

"Well, I guess I've gotta go."

"No, no, you don't."

"Yes, I do. I wish I could make you see that."

"Well, I guess this is it then... Take care of yourself, Mary."

"You too, Todd."

They looked at each other for a long time. Each thinking this might be the last time they would see one another. Then Marion hugged Todd as hard as she could, and they held the embrace for a long time till Noah's impatient car horn blasted again, as if it were an extension of its owner's irritation.

Marion started to release her hold when Todd drew her back and said softly into her ear, "...Marion...I love you." She drew back and looked deep into his eyes. *Yes, He did... and she loved him.*

She let go, and suppressed an almost overwhelming urge to breakdown and cry, then turned away from him without a word and walked away. She took a half a dozen steps and paused to look back. Todd stood there still as a stone for a moment, then said in a coarse whisper just barely loud enough for her to hear, *"Don't go."*

She looked at him one last time, then turned around quickly and got into Noah's car. It cranked up and drove away, leaving Todd standing where he had been. He remained motionless for a long while, *except for the single tear which ran slowly down his cheek.*

CHAPTER ELEVEN

"The new incubators were installed a week ago last Thursday and the rest of ya animals should be in the day after tomorrow," said Allen Kirby-Smythe in his thick Yorkshire accent.

"I was told everything was to be in place when I arrived," said Noah Little, annoyed.

"I'm sorry, Dr. Little, but we had a wee bit of a problem with the contractors. It took longer than we figured for the new cage room," said Kirby-Smythe, pointing towards the wire structures at the far end of Little's new Cambridge laboratory. He led the way inside while Noah and Marion followed.

Dr. Allen Kirby-Smythe was a beanpole of a man: very tall and very skinny, about forty-five years of age. He had a closely trimmed grey beard which matched the hair atop his head in color only. The shaggy mop was rather long and unruly by comparison.

"...We did get ya ape," Dr. Kirby-Smythe continued, "...and a nasty little bugger he is too. Nearly took my bloody finger off, he did." Kirby-Smythe pointed to a chimpanzee that seemed to understand that the man was regaling to his visitors the tale of their first meeting. The animal seemed highly amused. "...Name's *Cheetah*...ya know, like in *Tarzan the Ape-man.*"

"Cheetah? ...*My that's original*," Marion commented.

"All ya files be in the closet yonder. Maybe ya assistant might like to start organizing them. Miss ah, Miss ah?..."

"Grand, Marion Grand."

Kirby-Smythe's expression softened a bit. "...Grand...Grand...Ya wouldn't be any relation to Dr. Alec Grand, now, would ya, love?"

"...He's my grandfather."

"Ah! Small world it is. Fine man ya grandfather, I've admired his work for years... Now, Dr. Little you and ya lovely assistant here will basically have the place to yourself this summer. We don't have much of a summer semester these days. So, 'course, ya won't have any teaching duties, or any other obligations for that matter. So, you're free to do whatever it is ya came here to do. If I can be of any help to ya just give me a jingle.

Oh! I do hope ya and Miss Grand here will be my guest for a little soiree I'm throwing at my country place a fortnight from Friday."

Noah looked at Marion, and then back to the Englishman. "Thank you, Dr. Kirby-Smythe, but I'm afraid we must decline. We're going to be quite busy, what with setting up the laboratory and everything--."

"Nonsense! *All work and no play* - don't ya know. Now, I simply refuse to take no for an answer. A rather informal get together it'd be; just a few folk from the department: Dr. Rollins, Dr. Marsh, Professor Altman, a few others, and their wives, of course. It'd give ya a chance to sample a little *British hospitality*. Do ya ever ride horses, Miss Grand?"

Marion smiled and started to gain a little enthusiasm for the prospect. "Why, yes, I do."

"So, it's all settled then. You and Dr. Little must stay the weekend. There be plenty of room for ya at *Rangley Hall,* and I'm sure the both of you'll fall for the place same as me and my Jenny. Well, then, I'll send my car around for ya 'bout five o'clock two weeks from this Friday."

Kirby-Smythe offered his hand to Little. Noah shook it and said, "Dr. Kirby-Smythe, you are a very persuasive man. We have been working very hard of late. Perhaps a small respite would be in order. Thank you very much for your gracious invitation. We accept."

Kirby-Smythe, Noah and Marion all made good their farewells. Kirby-Smythe left, and Noah and Marion set to work unpacking. Marion was hoping for a brief vacation and perhaps a little sight-seeing. *Such would not be the case.* A week after their arrival at Cambridge it was difficult to find any noticeable difference from the routine they had left behind - *just longer lab hours.*

She began to count the days till their visit to *Rangley Hall.*

*****

Marion rose that Friday morning anticipating the short holiday with alacrity reminiscent of her *pre-Noah Little days.* She set about her morning tasks almost singing. It was the most joy Noah had allowed into her life since he had enslaved her. He even seemed to be treating her with a bit more dignity.

"I didn't know you rode horses," Noah said as he checked the setting on one of the culture incubators.

Marion was sitting on the floor with boxes of documents flanking her to either side, and stacks of file folders of assorted sizes arrayed before her. She looked over her glasses at him. "I beg your pardon?"

"...I said, I didn't know you rode horses."

"Yeah. When I was a teenager, I even used to show."

"Oh really. I used to work at a stable after school when I was a little boy. Dad being the vet and all; he got me the job. The manager's daughter and I would ride the trails on Saturdays... *Humph,* I haven't thought of that in years."

Marion looked at the reflective expression on his

face. At that moment, somehow he didn't seem so bad. It seemed impossible to conceive, but there had even been a time when she had actually liked him. "That sounds nice, Noah."

For the first time in nearly a month, he smiled at her. "Maybe this weekend you and I could take a ride together."

"...I'd like that, Noah."

"Well, we better get some of this work caught up or we won't be able to go anywhere," said Noah, returning to his usual *all business* manner.

*****

Marion worked like a demon the entire day and finished most of the filing, leaving behind four meticulously organized file cabinets, and dozens of empty cardboard boxes. She had worked hard and it showed in her tired face and her dirty clothes.

When she entered the cage room she found Noah preparing to give Cheetah an injection.

"Quittin' time, boss," she said in a former joviality. "...We need to get back to the barn so I can blast a few layers of this crud off-a-me before we head up to *Rangley Hall*."

Noah put the plastic top back over the syringe's needle and dropped it into the pocket of his lab coat, then hung the coat on a coat rack at the end of the room.

"Marion, I've been thinking...I believe with the amount of work that is left to be done we can ill afford both of us taking off this weekend. I'll take a taxi home and leave you the car, and then you can finish up your filing and get an early start tomorrow inoculating these animals. I'll go to Dr. Kirby-Smythe's and get this *little welcome to the neighborhood formality* over with so we'll be shed of him."

"Noah!" Marion exclaimed, disappointment radiating from her face like a flare.

Little looked at her very harshly.

Marion realizing that she had overstepped her place, started again in a less menacing tone, "Noah, I was really looking forward to this trip. I've been working some pretty long hours and I think I need a break."

"No, Marion, you *want* a break; you don't *need* a break, and you are old enough for your *wants* not to hurt you."

"Noah!" she said raising her voice, and then lowering it again, "...I'm not a machine. I need to rest from time to time."

"Marion, I don't think you're being a team player here." Noah considered a moment, and then sighed. "Oh, very well then, I suppose there is some merit in what you are saying. You may have Sunday off. - Of course, that is provided you've finished all the filing and have injected all the test animals."

"Noah, I don't think you're being fair. I think--"

"I am not interested in what you think," Noah said roughly, interrupting,"...and as for being fair - well, you already know my views on being fair. I've spoken on the matter, and that's the end of it."

Marion started to protest further, but Noah's resolute glare prevented it.

"Now, mind what I say. I should be extremely disappointed if your assignments were not completed on my return... *extremely*."

With that Noah left. Marion returned to the small stack of files which remained atop her desk, then suddenly threw them up into the air in a fit of blind anger, sending hundreds of sheets of paper flying everywhere. She sat down to cool off. *If she had had a gun, she would have shot Noah Little dead right on the spot.* But she didn't, so she settled for picking up her mess. She began to laugh, and then said aloud with bitter irony, "I guess *Cinderella won't be going to the ball after all*."

CHAPTER TWELVE

Rangley Hall turned out to be about the most impressive private residence Noah had ever been a guest. Obviously, Allen Kirby-Smythe was privy to quite a bit more capital than his salary from the Cambridge University afforded him. Contrary to what his almost cockney accent would first lead one to believe, he was apparently from old money. This was witnessed by the large, rambling, 300 year old manor house, which Kirby-Smythe had proudly informed Noah, had been in his family for over three generations. The house was almost a museum of expensive art and rare books, and its early Victorian furniture seemed to look like things you would be afraid to sit on. Noah kept expecting to see red velvet ropes cordoning off restricted areas.

The invited guests turned out to be an elegant group, all very friendly, but all very properly *blue blood*. Noah Little felt rather intimidated - *a feeling to which he was not accustomed.*

"Tell me, Dr. Little, what sort of research are you planning to do here at our little university?" asked Dwight Altman, professor of pharmacology.

Noah regarded Professor Altman. He was a short fat, balding man, who always seemed to be lighting a pipe.

"Cancer research, Professor Altman, I'll be doing cancer research," answered Little.

"Call me Dwight. Any particular area, or is it just cancer in general. Surely, there is a specific form you have in mind, mmm?"

Noah coughed as the smoke from Altman's pipe began forming a cloud around his head making his eyes water. "*Lung cancer*, Professor Altman, *lung cancer*."

"Dr. Little, where is the girl?" asked Kirby-Smythe, appearing out of nowhere.

"Miss Grand sends her apologies. I'm afraid she became ill rather suddenly today," Noah answered politely.

"Nothing serious, I hope."

"No, nothing serious. *Migraines*. She has them from time to time. They're quite painful. Poor girl; they do seemed to happen upon her unexpectedly."

"That's too bad. Maybe she can join us some other time."

"I'm sure she would like that very much."

Kirby-Smythe turned to Altman and said beaming, "And a right fair figure of a woman that one is, Miss Grand."

"Is she now?" said Altman.

"Yes, that she is, Dwight. It's a pity she's not here, it is."

Just then two more men entered the room where Kirby-Smythe stood behind the bar serving up drinks to Noah and Altman. One was sort of nondescript: middle aged, average height and build. The other man was much older, and almost a cartoon caricature of the stereotypical psychiatrist; *even down to the goatee.*

"Ah! Bob, Sean, good of you to come. Come meet our new friend from the *colonies*," called Kirby-Smythe, brimming over with good fellowship. He introduced nondescript, then *goatee* to Noah.

"This here be Bob Rollins, and me ole pal Sean Marsh. Gentlemen, meet Noah Little"

Noah shook hands with Rollins, then Marsh.

"It's a pleasure, sir," said Rollins

"Noah Little. Aye, ye reputation proceeds ya", said Marsh in a large Scottish brogue, "...How fortunate it is for us to be havin' such a noted scholar amongst us."

"You're too kind, Dr. Marsh," said Noah doing a fair imitation of humility.

Marsh noticed the drink in Noah's hand. "...*And drinkin' Scotch yet!* I like ye already, Mister Little."

"Well, now, gentleman, what'll it be this evening: chess? ...cards? ...billiards?" offered Kirby-Smythe.

Noah finished off his drink and said with a little anticipation, "...*Pool?*"

*****

Marion slammed the drawer of the file cabinet closed and tried to look on the bright side. *At least she would have a few days without Noah Little.* She realized that she had grown to hate him. She had never really hated anyone in her life before; not really. But she did now. *She hated Noah Jonas Little.*

She was about ready to call it a night when she came across a box marked: "PERSONAL". It was a box that was supposed to have been off-loaded into Noah's office, but was set off with the others in the main lab by mistake.

She opened the box. Inside were many framed certificates, citations and degrees, but it was four books that captured her curiosity. One was a book called *Hitler's Master Race*, one was titled: *Ethnic Purity,* one she found to her utter astonishment had been written by her grandfather called: *The Devolution of Mankind,* and last but not least, was *the handwritten scientific journal of one Dr. Noah Little.*

Marion couldn't believe her good luck. After browsing through the journal she found parts of it were almost a diary. *She always knew there had to be a book like this somewhere.* Someone as secretive as Noah just had to confide in someone or he would explode, even if it were only the blank pages of a notebook. She turned the journal to its beginning. The first entry was only a little more than a year old. Before the night was over at last - *she would have answers!*

*****

"...All night long I've listened to all of you humanists talking about the noble semi-divine nature of man. Given the proper set of circumstances the heathen will always sink to his lowest level. I'm sure you chaps read about that ball team whose plane crashed in the Andes. A grizzly tale that one. When they ran outta provisions *they started to eat one another*. Ghastly!" said Altman as he chalked his cue stick and prepared to shoot.

"Aye, but to be sure, Dwight you're leavin' out the real crux of da matter. Here were these lads atop this great mountain smack in the middle of the Andes, with no food, no radio - everyone had given 'em up fa dead. And it wasn't like they were killin' one another. There were already dead bodies all around the bloody plane! - All frozen solid like they were in a meat locker. They did what they had ta, man," said Marsh.

"I would have never been able to have done that. *There are worst things than death.* I don't think a civilized, God fearin' Christian could sink to cannibalism," remarked Altman, indignantly.

Kirby-Smythe poked a finger into Altman's formidable belly and said, "Dwight, but ya wouldn't have ta. Ya could live off ya own blubber more-than-a year!"

Everyone laughed but Altman, who blushed with embarrassment.

"Besides, Altman, you don't know what you'd do in a

situation like that. None of us do till we're faced with it," added Rollins.

The cue ball made a loud clatter as it struck the twelve ball sending it and several others flying about the billiard table. "I agree with Professor Altman," Noah said as he leaned over the table to take another shot. All turned to Noah in surprise, for he had not once contributed to the prolonged discussion in which the rest of Kirby-Smythe's guests had been involved.

"Ah, Dr. Little, please; a fresh perspective. We would love to hear ya views," invited Kirby-Smythe.

"Yes, by all means," from Altman; sensing a possible advocate."

Noah leaned on his cue stick and began:

"I'm sorry to say I've never been much of a practitioner of organized religion, so, the term *heathen* is really not quite applicable to my line of reasoning, but I can draw a parallel.

I find that there are basically two kinds of people in the world: *the principled and the unprincipled.*

And the unprincipled can always be counted upon to sink to their lowest - *like an animal.* There are those who strive for a loftier plane of being, and there are those who are only interested in gratifying their own immediate wants and desires. So, in other words, we have two men walking down the same road: one looks at the horizon, while the other looks at his feet. Therefore, one sees the sky, and the other sees only the dusty road beneath his foot. One dreams of the clouds; the other is consumed with the bare mundane mechanics of walking; something he does by instinct - *like an animal.*

Professor Altman claims that if he had been among those who had survived that crash he would have accepted death before compromising an ideal. So, Professor Altman by doing so proves himself a man of principle rather than an animal. And as we are all biologically animals: principle is the only thing that really distinguishes us from an orangutan."

"Yes, but as I said before, none of us can be sure what we would do in a certain situation until in fact we are faced with that situation in real life," said Rollins, "...Professor Altman can hypothesize all day long about what he would do or would not do in a hypothetical situation but - that's all it is... *an hypothesis*.

If Dwight here would have in fact been apart of that ill-fated band of young men, and when push came to shove - *ate human flesh*; I would not think the less of him."

"And I think ye are all being too hard on the poor lads," interjected Marsh, "...To be callin' 'em *heathens* is a might too harsh. I'ma good a Christian as the next man, and I read the book of their account. And a right spiritual thing it was too. I dare say those boys that come down outta the Andes have a more profound faith in the Almighty than any of us will ever know.

And what they did wasn't immoral. What we really are is of the *spirit*. Our bodies are just vehicles that our *spirits* ride around in. They did what they had ta, and they weren't eatin' *human beings,* they were eatin' *human bodies - and there be quite a bit of difference 'tween the two."*

"So, you're saying *the end justifies the means?*" queried Altman.

"Well...in this case - aye," answered Marsh.

"I believe the end **always** justifies the means," said Noah coming back into the conversation, and apparently switching sides. "The good of the collective majority is always paramount. Individual lives are expendable."

"Now, I'll never go along with that!" exclaimed Altman.

"Let me ask you this, Professor Altman," began Noah confidently, "...if you could go back in time to the day of Adolph Hitler's birth, and walk right up to his cradle and pull out a gun and blow him back to hell. *Would you do it?"*

"...Well, I suppose I would...yes I would - most definitely."

"So, you see you prove my point. The death of one individual would prevent the slaughter of millions. One individual's life would be expendable. But let's say after you did the deed you would be branded a monster; a heartless fiend who murdered an infant child in cold blood. Knowing that history would remember you only as a monster, and not the savior of all those destined to be killed in World War II, *would you still pull the trigger?"*

Altman pondered the scenario for a long time then said simply, "Yes."

"Again you choose to sacrifice the individual; in this case, your own life, for the good of the collective majority - proving you are a man driven by *principle* rather then mere animal instinct. Also, you prove my other point: *the end justifies the means.* By murdering a helpless infant in cold blood you save millions of lives and untold destruction."

The assembled group was silent; contemplating the philosophy which Noah was outlining. They were hard pressed to find a flaw in it. Noah was just getting warmed up. He went on:

"...I said before that I thought there were only two kinds of people in the world; *the principled and the unprincipled,* and I think I've demonstrated that *the end justifies the means.* Let's take it a step farther. I put it to you gentleman. Every great civilization since the dawn of man has been brought down by *the unprincipled*. What if there was a way to separate the *principled* from the *unprincipled?* And eradicate the *unprincipled*. Imagine if you will a world without addicts, child abusers, drug dealers or criminals of any sort."

"Yeah, but Mister Little, who's gonna be the one who'll be decidin' whose *principled* and who hain't. It sounds like ya tryin' to play God," opposed Marsh.

"And you're leaving out the possibility of a man seeing the error of his ways and repenting," added Altman.

"But what if there was a way to put the *unprincipled* in a position where they would destroy themselves through their own wickedness, without bringing down the innocent?" responded Little.

Kirby-Smythe had had enough of the serious mood his party had taken on, and asked laughingly, "To be sure, Dr. Little, and *if a bullfrog had wings he wouldn't bump his ass when he hopped,* would he now?"

*****

It was slightly past six in the morning when Marion Grand slammed the cover shut on Noah Little's journal. She had skimmed through the other books, and had mostly read the journal from cover to cover. She had read non-stop all night long. Now, she sat at her desk in her small office trembling, as the meaning of what she had read began to sink in.

Noah Little had logical reasons and substantiated facts for the conclusions he had reached, and on paper they made sense. But it was too *machine-like*; totally pragmatic. There was not an ounce of humanity or compassion in his theories or proposals, just soulless conjecture drawn from raw data... But somehow it had all been taken out of context. If you had to point to a particular area and say *this is wrong*, or to a certain spot and say this was *not right* - you couldn't, but every fiber of your being told you that the whole thing was dreadfully *WRONG*. If you had to explain why it was wrong, the best you could do was say *...Because it just is!*

Noah began his theories with a premise of why he thought civilizations rose and fell. He said that civilizations were begun by people of vision and great strength. They had to be physically and psychologically sound. There were no weak or emotionally crippled individuals at the beginning of a society, because long before the foundations of that society had been laid, those people would have been killed off through natural selection. *Only the strong survived.* There were no lazy people either, because basically, *if you didn't work - you starved.* The founders of a civilization started with raw earth and rose to the challenge of building a nation. At the beginning, everyone was highly motivated and enthusiastic. At this point ends the first stage. In later stages that motivation and enthusiasm would slowly erode.

The second stage begins when a highly motivated lower class decides that it wants what the upper class has. Then there is usually a civil war...or two...or three. If the civilization survives the civil wars it enters into the third stage.

The third stage begins when the lower class has gained enough ground to where it begins to become satisfied with what it has been allotted.

Noah stopped at this point to define what being satisfied meant. He wrote, *"Human greed will always want just a little bit more, so, in that respect no one will ever be truly contented. However, being satisfied is the point in which a person's discontentment is less than his willingness to expend the energy to make a change.*

*Poverty is relative. If you are content with little you are always satisfied. But there is a line that separates slavery from mere low wages. A slave has nothing to lose, **so, he revolts.** If a low paid factory worker is paid just enough to get by, **fear of unemployment** will keep him from upsetting the status quo.*

There is however a variable to account for: the threshold at which a person reaches their point of contentment varies from individual to individual, but the average person's point of contentment is fairly low. If this were not the case everyone would be a millionaire. Of course, keep in mind these are generalities, there will always, always be exceptions. There are no absolutes when dealing with individual people, however this satisfaction/contentment threshold concept will consistently hold true with LARGE masses..."

Noah's third stage of civilization painted a picture of a people who had become complacent. They had built their society. Everyone overall was fairly comfortable, or at least to the point where *they had more to lose than to gain by revolting.* The elite felt secure in their power and authority, and the lower classes had enough to prevent them from rioting. But there were no great challenges to meet. They had vanquished all their enemies, built all the roads and cities, reconciled their civil wars, and had for all intents and purposes, *plopped down on the couch to drink beer and eat potato chips until they had grown so fat and lazy they couldn't move.* At this stage of the game neighboring kingdoms came in and slaughtered them like beached whales. This was up to present day history where Noah claimed all the great civilizations had died.

Modern times brought a new circumstance. Noah explained that the advent of atomic warfare had stagnated the cycle. If an atomic war were waged everyone instinctively knew there could be *no winner.* Therefore, other than third world skirmishes, all out world war was not feasible.

Now, Noah described the fourth and final stage of civilization. Medical science had advanced to the point where people lived longer, and fell prey to fewer and fewer terminal illnesses. All things considered, it would naturally follow that there would have to be larger and larger populations because there would be no great wars or disease to periodically wipe out the overgrowth. *Mankind was becoming like a large tree in need of pruning.* If something wasn't done, it would become so large that it would not be able to take in enough substance to keep itself alive. The diseased limbs would bring about the death of the whole tree: *diseased and healthy.*

As society matured it began to feel a moral obligation to take care of those who could not take care of themselves. This was in drastic contradiction with basic laws of nature. In the animal kingdom there were *no manic depressive buffalos.* There were no *Bengal tigers walking around with triple by-passes.* When animals were born defective they simply didn't survive. In modern human society this was not the case. Not only did they survive, they proliferated, passing on their congenital defects to subsequent generations - *thus contaminating the collective gene pool.*

Government social programs actually encouraged the growth of substandard gene pools. Noah cited several experiences he had had while working at inner-city hospitals where he had met women whom he had termed, *baby machines.* These were women who had had broods of children; some as large as ten, whose ages were in successive intervals of one year apart. *These women had these children every year so they could increase their welfare allotments.*

The final nail in the coffin of the forth stage of civilization, Noah explained, was drug abuse. The breeding of substandard genetic material was bad enough left alone, but was set into hyperspace by the chromosome damage the use of narcotics and hallucinogens left behind.

Devoid of the enthusiasm to make the sacrifices necessary to achieve in mainstream society, and also hampered with substance addictions and low intelligence, (partly from their lack of educational opportunities, and partly from defects in their genetic makeup) the lower segments of the populace grew disillusioned...*then bitter*.

To feed their drug addictions they turned to crime. As man is inherently a social creature, urban tribes were formed whose business became *criminal*. These urban tribes were made up of those who would not, or could not be accepted elsewhere, and as its members could not live by accepted values, *they evolved their own*.

Complete subcultures were formed by these social outcasts with codes, rituals, and even territorial warfare, *(with the government picking up the medical bills for their casualties)*. Finally, these urban tribes eventually grew so large; they surpassed the ability of law enforcement to control.

Noah believed that the urban tribes would continue to grow larger and larger and would become more and more contaminated. The inbreeding and drugs would eventually evolve them into something less than apes, and they would become so large a population that they would destroy modern society, and would absorb all of thinking mankind.

Morality kept society from recognizing its impending doom, and even if it did, that same morality would keep it from doing anything about it.

The words written in Noah Little's journal portrayed a man obsessed. He was outraged by the future he saw for his species. Page after page of statistics on population growth, teenaged pregnancies, drug addiction and drug related crime filled whole sections of the journal. Column after column of figures began to take on disturbing significance as their multiplying geometries began to add up to *genocide*. If Noah Little's math was correct, the total breakdown of society and the complete devolution of mankind was scarcely... *one hundred and thirty five years away*.

It was in the midst of his deepest despair over this revelation that a plan emerged in his mind that would offer salvation to the human race. It was a project he had dubbed... *Weed Killer*.

CHAPTER THIRTEEN

It was drizzling rain when Kirby-Smythe's Bentley drove up into the driveway of Little's brownstone.

Noah noticed the gray BMW parked out front and thought of Marion. *He began to feel a touch of guilt.* He began to think perhaps he had been wrong; *maybe he should have let her come with him for the weekend.*

The luxurious automobile rolled to a stop, then Kirby-Smythe's driver got out and retrieved Noah's small suitcase from the boot of the car, and then opened the door for Noah to egress. Noah got out and led the driver up to the house, took the overnight case from him, mumbled a vague thank you, then went inside, closing the door in the driver's face.

*****

"Marion?" he called to the empty house. "Marion!" he bellowed, walking about the huge apartment looking for her. "Marion," he called a third time, and was still greeted by silence. *Where was she?*

He went upstairs. "Marion!" He walked into the bedroom - *no Marion.* This was a puzzle. The car was out front. *Where could she have gone without it? "She wouldn't have gone for a walk, not in this weather,"* he thought to himself.

He descended the stairs to the kitchen, brewed a pot of coffee and fixed himself a sandwich. With the coffee made, he took a cup and the sandwich into the den to sit down before the television. The program did not amuse him. He never could develop a taste for the British sense of humor. He switched off the set. *Where is that woman?*

He took his dirty plate back into the kitchen, dropped it into the sink, refilled his coffee cup and returned to the den. This time he played *Chopin* on the stereo, and settled down with a book in his easy chair.

Soon he lost himself in its pages and time slipped by unnoticed.

He looked at his watch: 11:30 P.M. *This was peculiar.*

"Well, she had better have gotten those test animals injected or young Miss Grand will be finding herself in a great deal of trouble come tomorrow," Noah mused angrily.

He went upstairs, undressed, put on his pajamas, turned out the lights, and got into bed. *Where is that damn woman?!* Soon he was fast asleep.

*****

Noah's eyes sprang open. There had been a sound ...*or had there?* He closed his eyes again. *Was there someone in the room with him?* He quickly rose up in the bed to look around - *nothing.*

"Marion?" he called out into the dark room.

No reply.

He looked around. Nothing moved. He listened. All was silent. He lay back down in the bed and stared at the ceiling for some fifteen minutes. Then sleep took him again.

Something touched the mattress. He opened his eyes and sprang full awake. He saw her standing above him, wild eyed and frightening, *holding a small hatchet.* **It was Marion!**

She screamed like a banshee as she brought the hatchet down with all her might straight for his face. Noah rolled off the other side of the bed and fell onto the floor with a loud thud as the hatchet buried itself into the pillow.

A terrified Noah Little scrambled awkwardly to his feet and frantically scanned the room for his attacker. He saw nothing in the eerie shadows. He cautiously made his way to the light switch. *Had it been a dream?* He clicked on the light. Feathers from the down pillow floated in the air, and there was a savage gash in the pillow where just moments ago his head had been.

Footsteps ran across the carpet in the hallway outside. Noah tiptoed out into the hall and then carefully went around to all the rooms on the top floor, flipping on light switches as he went. Then suddenly, the hatchet came flying from the direction of the bathroom, and stuck into the wall mere inches in front of his face.

At first fear filled his chest like it had been poured from a hot caldron, and then it was instantly replaced with molten fury. *She was in the bathroom!*

He stormed through the door without a thought, which proved to be almost fatal. Noah did not expect the blurry form of the wiry little woman to be charging him straight on with a large pair of dressmaker's scissors raised above her head. If he had deflected its course but a second later, the scissors would have plunged into his heart, rather than going up to the handles into his left shoulder. Noah howled with agonizing pain. Never in his entire life had he experienced anything that remotely approached pain of such magnitude. He instinctively backhanded Marion Grand with all his strength sending the woman crashing into the large bathroom mirror where it exploded, sending thousands of shards of glass loudly spraying in all directions. When all the clatter had ceased - *she was gone.*

The bathroom was lit only by the light coming in from the hallway. Noah didn't see the remnants of the broken mirror on the floor in front of him, neither did he think about his bare feet till he started to run out of the room. The broken glass savagely bit his feet like hungry piranha. He again howled with pain as he gingerly hopped out into the hallway, and then hurriedly headed for his bedroom leaving bloody footprints behind. Once he got there he slammed the door shut and locked it.

He jumped with a frightful start when he first noticed the scissor handles sticking out of his shoulder, and gave a low involuntary shriek. When he turned to the vanity mirror, the image he saw horrified him. His pajama shirt was drenched in blood, and its whole left shoulder was a dark crimson; the protruding handles pulsating rhythmically with his pounding heart.

He saw the bloody footprints leading to where he was standing reflected in the mirror. He whirled around to see them with his own eyes hoping that the mirror had somehow been lying. *It hadn't.* He then looked down at his lacerated feet and for the first time realized that *they hurt like hell.* As he looked at his feet he noticed the scissors again, and then jerked around causing excruciating spasms of pain to ripple across his chest as he saw the blades protruding from his back a good half an inch.

He scrambled as fast as his injuries would permit to the phone. When he picked up the receiver... *there was no dial tone.*

"Calm down," he thought to himself. *"I've got to calm down and think!"* His breathing and heart rate were racing. He sat down on the bed and as the adrenaline began to wear off, he slowly began to think methodically:

"Marion has lost her mind. Why, I don't know. And I don't have time to worry about that now. I've got to think...think...gotta be rational.

Okay now, be logical... be logical. Now, what is the situation? I'm locked in a house with a mad woman who's trying to kill me. The phone is dead. - She must have done something to it. I can't call for help. What am I going to do? What am I going to do?..." Noah began to panic again.

He started to breathe hard. Then with effort, he forced himself to be steady and regained his head.

"I'm hurt. Should I try to pull these scissors out? No, that's no good! If I pull them out the bleeding will get worse. I've got to get to a hospital.

I'll sneak outside, get the car and drive to the hospital and then I'll call the police and they'll put that crazy bitch under the jail... No, that's no good either she's got the fucking car keys...No neighbors!...I'm trapped!...I've gotta get out...DAMMIT! I gotta DO SOMETHING!

But what? What am I going to do? ...Well, whatever it is I'm gonna have to do it myself. And I better be pretty damn quick about it before that Amazon bitch breaks the damned fucking door down!

All right, all right, first things first, I can't fight her in this condition. I'm gonna have to do something about these scissors. My medical bag! Oh, God, please let it be in the closet!"

Noah bolted to his feet and the pain from the sudden movement nearly brought him to his knees. He went to the closet and found the black leather satchel he was looking for and opened it. *He had been fortunate.* It was a very well stocked emergency kit, containing all sorts of bandages, disinfectants, surgical instruments, and the greatest prize of all - *a local anesthetic.*

CHAPTER FOURTEEN

The woman hung over the toilet and threw up. As she had eaten very little in the last few days, it was mostly the dry heaves. *Had she killed him?* She tried to remember. *No, she had not.* She remembered that she had wounded him pretty severely, but she also remembered him running into the bedroom.

There was a phone in the bedroom! She grabbed her hatchet and ran out of the house. It was dark and pouring rain outside. *Telephone poles? Where were they?* She found them, and then followed their wires to where they were attached to the side of the house. She took aim with her hatchet and started to swing, then stopped abruptly. *Was that the phone wire, or was it the electrical line?* **She didn't know.** She looked at her wet clothes and wiped her long wet hair from her eyes as the rain and wind blasted her from behind. *She didn't know the difference.* If it was the electric line and she chopped into it with her hatchet, she would instantly be electrocuted. On the other hand, if he was upstairs calling the police - it would all be over anyway. She closed her eyes and gave a mighty swing... *the phone lines fell to the ground.*

*****

Noah Little had always thought of himself as something of *cosmic significance*. Marion Grand, on the other hand, had never thought that she would play a vital role in the destiny of mankind, and never could have imagined a day would come when she would be in Cambridge England, standing outside in the pouring rain with her whirling mind desperately trying to devise a way to murder her boss. She never thought she would have had the guts. She never thought that she would have had the strength to do what she had just attempted. *But she had failed* - THREE TIMES! However, she knew she couldn't give up now. The lives of over a billion people depended on her success.

She had reached the point of no return now. She had to follow through with the decision she had made yesterday. There could be no turning back now. In a person's life at some point they reach a fork and a decision has to be made which defines the shape of the rest of that life. It had been just a little less than two days previous that Marion Elizabeth Grand stood at her crossroads. Down one fork lay a rewarding life as a respected physician and research scientist, down the other was a life in prison, or even... *death.*

*****

Forty three hours before her third unsuccessful attempt to kill Noah Little, Marion Grand had sat in her office contemplating project *Weed Killer*. It would work. Of that there was no doubt in her mind whatsoever. The virus was absolutely perfect for the job it had been designed to do. All that remained was to develop a way to store it in a crystallized form where it could remain inert until it could be injected into its unsuspecting victims, then nature would take it from there. Once the fuse was lit, in slightly less than fifty years, one third of the population of earth would be exterminated.

She had to get out of the lab. She left the building and walked along the sidewalks of the campus trying to decide what to do.

She now knew they were in the final stages of *Weed Killer*. They had come to England to develop the stasis crystals. It wouldn't take long. They had almost had it before they had closed the stateside lab. Now that they could work at it full time it would be only a matter of time... *a short time.*

Marion sat down on a bench, closed her eyes and

tried to imagine the faces of a billion people. Then she realized that she would be partly responsible for their deaths. She thought of all the stumbling blocks that she herself had personally removed in Little's diabolical scheme. *No wonder he wouldn't let her go* - he had come to need her. It wasn't her body... *it was her mind.*

Over the past months he had used all those sadistic, psychological tortures to break her will! It was so clear now. *"The son of a bitch was brainwashing me just like Todd said,"* Marion said aloud to herself.

For some minutes she became so angry that she couldn't think straight. She jumped up and started walking again. When her temper had begun to simmer a bit, she started to reason more clearly.

She had to hand it to him; he was a genius. He had set a goal, then manipulated people, institutions and even nature itself without their knowledge to achieve what he had set out to do. Now, he stood at the very brink of victory. *Could she stop him? Possibly.* But then she asked herself... *should she?*

What if Noah was right? If she could stop him she would save over a billion lives in the short term, but would destroy the whole of civilization in the long term. Would it be better to sacrifice a third of mankind in a cold calculated extermination, or leave it to its own devices and let it completely destroy itself.

She shuttered. *Who was she to make a decision like that?* She was just a student; not yet thirty years old. But she also knew that Noah would implement his plan and multitudes of people would perish. Then she realized to her chagrin, she was the only person on the planet who stood in a position to prevent it.

...But he WAS wrong. She had no facts or statistics to prove it, but everything in her being told her that he had

missed something. Maybe when the populations grew too large mankind would take to the stars, or maybe people would live under the sea. Somebody would come up with an answer. Somebody always had in the past. Somebody **would** in the future. She had faith that things would work out, and a belief in a Divine intervention in a way as of yet inconceivable. That was the difference between her and him. *Noah Little didn't have faith in anything.*

She hurried back to the science building and searched the offices until she found what she was looking for... *a large document shredder.*

The machine was on a rolling pedestal, and she purposefully wheeled the device into their laboratory. She plugged in the shredder, opened the top drawer of the file cabinet and removed the first file in the A section. When she had removed the last file from the Z section, there was an enormous pile of confetti on the floor, and the open drawers of Dr. Little's file cabinets where empty.

Marion then removed all the culture dishes from the incubators and lined them up in very neat tight rows on top of a rolling gurney. Then she wheeled the gurney up to their X-ray machine, set it at its highest intensity and widest dispersal, and then irradiated the cultures - NINE TIMES! When she had finished the procedure absolutely no life whatsoever survived.

After this, she deleted all the computer records by bulk erasing all the tapes and floppy discs. As an after thought, *just to be sure*, she tossed those into the shredder as well. Then for pure spite, she went out into the hall, retrieved a fire axe, and smashed the expensive computer into a million tiny pieces.

She went to the cage room next and removed a dart pistol from a glass case affixed to the wall. She loaded the gun and stared at Cheetah. "I'm sorry, boy, but I don't know if you have this damn thing or not, and I don't have time to test you. I can't risk someone using you to grow more cultures." She fired the gun.

The dart stuck into the chimp's right shoulder and he began to chatter loudly, and then quickly went to sleep. When the animal was unconscious she loaded him onto another rolling gurney. He was heavy. She had a great deal of difficulty. Once she had him on the gurney she wheeled him into a room where Noah had had installed a large tank of acid that he had planned to use to destroy infected test animals. She carefully placed the chimpanzee on the motorized pedestal, and then threw the switch that activated the mechanism which would lower him inside. When the acid touched the animal's skin a loud hissing sound ensued. When the body was submerged, the caldron began to bubble and to boil violently as Cheetah's flesh dissolved.

*****

Marion went back into her office and sat down at her desk. *Had she destroyed everything? Yes.* She couldn't think of anything else. The files, the computer records, the computer, the cultures, the animals: it had all been wiped out. That is, it had all been wiped out - *except for in the mind of Noah Little.*

He hadn't done anything illegal that she could prove. The very most she could hope for by exposing his plot would be to have him fired and branded a madman. She had set him back a few years by what she had just done, but she hadn't stopped him, *not by a long shot.*

If she exposed his scheme to the world no one would believe it. If there were people who did, and he was dismissed from the university and blackballed in the scientific community forever, he could still eventually succeed on his own. Noah Little was an enormously wealthy individual. He could buy all the equipment he needed out of his own pocket, and in several years, he could possibly be ready to go again.

Her heart began to pound in her chest as she was forced to accept the only possible solution... *she would have to KILL Noah Little!*

*****

Marion Grand absently tightened and loosened the grip on the hatchet she held, while hiding in the dark gloom of Noah Little's closet. Now, she began to wonder if she were actually capable of murdering someone, and especially in such a savagely brutal way, and with such a crude instrument yet. When it came down to it, *could she really bury a hatchet in a man's face?* It was hard enough for her to grasp becoming a murderess to begin with, *but did she have to become an axe murderess?*

She wished she had a gun. When she had reconciled herself to the necessity of killing Noah, she thought, *"This is fucking England; I can't just hop down to K-Mart and buy a 'Saturday night special' and a box of shells!"*

Deciding on a weapon had been difficult. She had rummaged around their Cambridge residence searching for a weapon, picking up this and that, and not finding anything suitable. Then she found herself in the gardener's tool shed in back of the huge brownstone. It was there she found and settled on *the hatchet.*

When the front door opened downstairs, she stopped breathing for a moment, as fear shot through her body like a screaming fire engine. "Marion?" came Noah's call from the first floor; muffled and faint. "Marion!" he called again. "Marion," he said a third time. There was a long pause. "Marion!" he bellowed, this time, louder and very close. Marion gripped the hatchet even tighter. She could hear her heart pounding in her ears. Then she heard footsteps. He was in the bedroom - *just outside the closet*

119

door! There was a long interval where there was no movement. Then she heard him sigh, and then his footsteps went away.

A long period of unmeasured time elapsed. Marion hadn't slept in over thirty hours - *she fell asleep.*

The closet door burst open and a flood of light exploded in Marion's face. She woke with a jump, and almost screamed. But she was well hidden in the dark recesses of the large walk-in closet and remained undetected.

Noah retrieved his pajamas from a built in chest of drawers, then closed the door, again plunging Marion into darkness.

In the pitch black of the dark closet it was difficult for Marion to judge the passage of time. She waited for what seemed to her to be a great deal in length, but she had no idea as to whether it had been two hours or ten minutes. She was scared. More so than she had ever been in her life all put together. *No! She couldn't go through with this! But she had to.*

She knew the lives of countless people were depending on her. She began to think of the man she knew as *Noah Jonas Little.* As a tinge of hate began to rear its head above her fear she realized that if it were possible for her to kill another human being, Noah Little, of all possible candidates, *would be the easiest.* She gathered her strength and opened the closet door a little to take a peek.

The room was dark but her eyes had adjusted well, and her night vision was good. She could make out most of the room's details in an eerie black and white. Noah laid in his bed sound asleep. The closet door was a sliding type, which rolled laterally on tracks in the floor and ceiling. She began to carefully slide the door open wider, and then suddenly it began to bind on something. The aperture had not yet grown large enough for her to escape. She began to tremble. *What now?*

She thought for a moment, and then slowly began to give the stuck door an increasing amount of pressure. It broke loose with a loud shutter. Noah began to toss in his bed. *Oh no! He's waking up!* Marion reflexively slammed the door shut, inadvertently sealing the closet with a loud thud.

She heard Noah stir. Then he called out, "Marion?" Heavy panic filled her chest. She stood still as a stone. To her ears her own breathing sounded as loud as a chainsaw. She held her breath for as long as she could, then took short, slow, and *silent*, periodic gasps of air.

She felt waves of relief when at last she heard him lie back down, and after what seemed to be an enormously long time, heard him begin to take regular deep breaths, just one notch short of snoring. *He was asleep again.*

She tried the door once more, this time it opened effortlessly. She observed his sleeping form, and then silently stalked up beside him. She raised the hatchet and prepared to split wide his skull. She hesitated, then lowered the hatchet to her side and began to imagine what it would look like. It was such a gory thing she was about to do. She started to tremble again. *She was losing her nerve.*

She went over the reasons in her mind again. *It was time.* She brought the hatchet up in front of her face and held it with both hands. As she brought her weapon into striking position, her thigh brushed lightly against the side of the bed, making the mattress shake slightly atop its box springs.

Noah's eyes sprang open. *He was awake!* She had to move fast. She brought the hatchet down with all the strength she could muster as she screamed at the top of her lungs. "NOOOOOOOOoooooooooooo!" Noah rolled off the other side of the bed in just the nick of time and hit the floor with a thud. The hatchet tore into the pillow and Marion was thrown off balance and fell long ways onto the bed. She could hear Noah scrambling around on the floor. *She had missed.* Now, the only thing she could think of was to run.

She ran out into the hallway and stopped for a second trying to decide which way to go. The light suddenly came on in the bedroom behind her, and she ran into the bathroom terror stricken. She was breathing hard now. Lights began to come on all over the top floor.

The light came on in the hall. She could see him through the open door of the bathroom, but he couldn't see her lost within its gloom. He turned to look down into the stairwell. His back was turned. *Now, was her chance.* She stepped into the hall. A board creaked under her foot. He began to turn in the direction of the sound. *No!* ...In panic she threw the hatchet at him like a tomahawk. It missed and stuck into the wall next to his head. *Damn!* He whirled around to look at the hatchet protruding from the wall in front of him. He hadn't seen her. She retreated back into the bathroom.

She could see him coming now. She flashed on the large scissors she used to cut her hair. *Where were they?!!* She groped around frantically in the semi-darkness. She found them just as he burst into the room. She lunged forward driving the large dressmaker's scissors into the dark form where she estimated its heart would be. It pushed her sideways and she felt the scissors sink deep into flesh. Noah howled like a wounded wolf. Then a hand struck her hard across the mouth knocking her sideways on top of the lavatory. Her head slammed into the mirror and ripples of pain radiated all over her skull as glass shattered and fell unseen all around her to the dark floor.

She ran out into the hall holding her throbbing head. There was a rattling of glass from the bathroom and a loud shriek, then footsteps on the carpet behind her. She began to run for the stairs expecting the footsteps to be in pursuit. She was about to quicken her pace when she heard the soft footfalls turn to the left. She looked over her shoulder, and not seeing anyone chasing her, stopped momentarily. The bedroom door slammed. When she got to the spot where she had thrown the hatchet at Noah, she found it, still stuck in the wall. She removed it, and took it with her as she retreated down the stairs.

When she reached the bottom she ran from room to room in blind terror. When she began to get hold of herself, she became extremely nauseous, and ducked into the bathroom to throw up. While she was in the bathroom she remembered that there was a telephone in the bedroom which Noah could use to call the police. As soon as she became aware of the possibility, she ran outside into the rain to cut the phone lines. When she had accomplished their demise, she came back into the house, and then cautiously ascended the stairs.

Her shoes were wet from where she had been outside in the rainstorm. They made a very detectable squishing sound. She frowned, then stepped out of her canvass boat shoes and removed her socks, leaving them on the floor. Afterwards she tiptoed her way down the hall to the bedroom door as silently as she could. *Was Noah dead... or unconscious?* She knew she had stabbed him with the scissors, but she had no idea how bad. She looked at the floor. There were bloody footprints leading from the bathroom to the bedroom. She looked at the bedroom door knob. She tried it - *it was locked.*

CHAPTER FIFTEEN

It had been a curious sensation to pull the scissors from his own body, and even seemed stranger to sew his own flesh together. The anesthetic from his medical kit had worked wonderfully. There had been very little pain, but he could feel the blades of the scissors move through his body as he pulled them free, and felt a weird tugging sensation as he stitched the entry wound closed awkwardly with one hand.

Of course, there was little he could do about the exit wound. Fortunately, it hadn't been too bad. All in all, it had looked a lot worse than it actually was. Miraculously, the contortions of the attacker and victim while struggling had sent the scissors in at an angle which had lodged it in between bone, and mainly punctured muscle. Movement of the arm would be stiff and a bit weaker, but until the local wore off, there would not be much pain.

When Noah had finished with the scissor wound, he wiped off most of the blood with his bed sheet, disinfected all his lacerations and bandaged them. After this, he went to the closet and put on a gunmetal gray warm up suit, and as he sat on the edge of his bed, carefully trying to coax a large loose fitting pair of bedroom shoes over his bandaged feet, *he heard someone try the locked bedroom door.*

He stared at the door for a long time. - *Silence.* Apparently, she had gone away. *He hoped.* He donned the shoes, got up, and turned over the nightstand, then stomped it to pieces, a somewhat painful operation with sore feet. Then with some difficulty, trimmed away from its wreckage a fairly stout club. *He was ready to do battle now. - It would be him or her.*

As soon as he emerged from the bedroom, the house went dark. He looked around, and fear seized his heart again. *It would not be easy. He would have to be very cautious. Marion Grand was dangerous.*

The fuse box was in the kitchen pantry. Knowing this, Noah reasoned that Marion had to be downstairs, so, he quietly descended. At the bottom he listened. He heard nothing. He made his way down the hall to the den. - No one there. Then to the kitchen ...then to the study... *Where was she?*

Suddenly, from the darkness came a blinding flash of light. Marion had set off the flash attachment of her 35mm camera right in Noah's face. He dropped his club; startled. Now, he was as blind as a stump.

For most people that would have been the end. Marion came at him with her hatchet. He was temporarily blinded and dazed. But Noah had steeled himself for the unexpected, and managed to keep his head. His mind took in the situation and moved like lightning. He dropped low and lunged forward catching Marion at the pit of her stomach with his good shoulder. Marion was not expecting the sudden move and lost her balance, flinging her small deadly axe out into the dark room.

Noah pushed forward and lifted up slightly, lofting the much smaller woman off her feet, then slamming her into the wall, sending framed photographs crashing to the floor. Noah couldn't see much yet, but his tackle maneuver had knocked the breath out of his opponent. She offered no resistance till Noah had pinned her to the wall, and his groping hands found their way around her throat.

He began to strangle her in a viselike grip as she tried futilely to pry his hands loose. *He was just too strong for her*. Her eyes bulged, her tongue began to stick out, and she began to feel her consciousness ebb. *NO!* ... She kneed him savagely in the groin, with all the power of a kicking mule.

"Ahgggggggggh!" yelled Noah, releasing his grip and

doubling over in pain. Marion ran from the room, while Noah fell to his knees: his face contorted in agony.

"DAMN YOU!" Noah screamed, as raging fury consumed him. He got to his feet and went after her. He caught up with her as she began to open the front door. He ran into her, shoving her face into the door; slamming it shut again with a loud bang. She gave a short scream. Noah grabbed her from behind, taking hold of her forehead and jaw, and gave it a powerful twist. *There was a very loud, sickening crack!* She fell limp in his arms. He let go and watched her slump to the floor. - It was over... *Marion Grand was dead.*

*****

The whine from the buffing machine echoed through the empty corridors as Noah wheeled a large blue trunk along on a hand truck he had borrowed from the janitor. The janitor smiled as Noah wheeled by and said something, but it was lost under the noise of his machine. Noah nodded and continued down the long twisting path through the science building to his laboratory. When he got to the door he fumbled for the right key, opened it, pushed the trunk inside and locked the door behind him.

At first he just stood there with his mouth open and then he went to the middle of the room and made a slow panorama, taking in the extent of its destruction.

"What have you done?" he asked in a raspy whisper. "WHAT - HAVE - YOU - DONE?!" he asked again, this time almost yelling. Then he collapsed wearily onto a tall stool. He shook his head in disbelief.

"Damn you... damn you to hell, Marion Grand! Look at what you've done..."

Noah sprang to his feet and started to walk around the wrecked laboratory. "Fool...you FOOL! ...Look what you've done. You've ruined everything!"

He picked up a hand full of confetti, looked at it, and then angrily threw it aside. He began to notice small pieces of plastic and glass scattered everywhere, and was confused as to where they had come from until he realized *the computer was gone*. He examined the empty incubators. *Where were the viral cultures?* After a brief search he found them under the X-ray machine. He knew what she had done; still he checked each one under a microscope. *They were all dead.*

What would he do now? He didn't know. She had destroyed everything. He felt numb. He would figure out something later but now... *he had a job to do.*

*****

Noah wheeled the large trunk up to the acid tank. *Where was the platform?* He went to the small control panel and hit the switch to raise the platform. He jumped in terror when he saw the skeleton sprawled out on the grated pedestal. He backed up against the wall. *Who is that?!*

"...*Wait ...that's not a human skeleton*," he said to himself, and then walked over to examine the remains more closely. "It's a chimpanzee.... Ooooooh." Noah rubbed his hand over his face and exhaled loudly then said aloud, "...Every contingency anticipated. *Amazing... simply amazing.*"

Noah put on a set of light blue coveralls and a thick pair of black insulated gloves, and then removed the skeleton from the platform. He put the bones in a very large aluminum basin affixed to the wall nearest the acid tank, then sprayed off the acid residue with a hanging high pressure water nozzle. Once Cheetah's remains were clean, he dropped them into a special rolling hamper where they would be disposed of by the university.

Noah opened the latches on the trunk and took a deep breath. *He hesitated.* He opened the trunk lid. Inside was the body of Marion Grand. It had taken on a bluish hue, and the eyes were still open. The face still had the same expression of terror upon its features as it had had during the last moment it was alive.

Noah removed the body and placed it on the pedestal above the acid tank. He went to the controls and paused to look at it one last time. *The eyes seemed to stare at him.* He flipped the switch and the sound of unseen motors broke the eerie silence of the room. Noah watched the pedestal lower Marion's body into the acid tank and heard the sizzle as her skin began to burn away. He watched the lifeless eyes stare at him as they disappeared into the bubbling, churning tank of acid, where he knew... *they would be no more.*

*****

Three weeks later Patti Meeks walked through the neat, orderly laboratory of Dr. Noah Jonas Little. Patti was a pretty young thing; blonde, tall, slender; just twenty two. She would be a pre-med student in the fall, and had been thrilled when Noah had hired her to be his new lab assistant.

"We've just got in that live viral culture from the *Devonshire Animal Clinic* you were expecting, Dr. Little," Patti Meeks informed in her sprightly British accent as she entered the open door of Noah's office.

Noah looked up from the work atop his desk and removed his glasses.

"Good, good... now, Miss Meeks, you recall the procedure I outlined yesterday about how I wanted the environments set on the culture incubators for the first three days?"

"Yes, sir."

"Well, those settings will be fine for that initial period, but after then they have to be increased two degrees Celsius, every four hours - *around the clock*. I'm afraid I'm going to have to ask you to work some strange hours for about a week or so."

"I understand, Dr. Little. No problem. Just be sure and keep *him* locked up in here if I gotta work at night."

"...Pardon me?"

"Him," said Patti grimacing, and pointing to the skeletal model which hung from a hook attached to a black, wrought iron stand that Noah had had made by one of the local artisans. "He gives me the willies," Patti said shuttering.

Noah regarded the skeleton and smiled weakly.

"That's not a *HIM*, Miss Meeks, that is a... that was a *HER*."

CHAPTER SIXTEEN

Out in the forest the sounds of various insects came wafting through the trees, punctuated now and then by the call of a bird. There were still several hours of daylight remaining, but the changing of the guard had begun: day creatures retiring, and night creatures awakening. From where he stood at the top of a long, but slight incline, he could see the campers and their counselors lining up in front of the cafeteria. There was a muffled commotion of laughter and talking from the assembled group of fifty or so, and the alluring aroma of spaghetti sauce floated on the breeze.

Todd Dillow was dressed in short pants and a *University of California* tee shirt. He held the end of a yellow ski rope which was threaded through the hands of six blind children, ranging in ages from nine to twelve: four girls and two boys. They had been hiking for several hours in the alpine countryside just outside of *The Lions Club Summer Camp for the Blind*, and were returning for dinner. *They were late.*

"Todd, you said we'd make it back before dinner," whined one of the boys.

"Dinner's not over... *so* … we did make it back before dinner," Todd said, letting his smile be heard in his voice.

"Yeah, but for cryin' out loud. We're gonna be at the end of the line," complained the other boy.

A tall skinny blonde girl took a deep breath and commented, "We're havin' spaghetti."

"I told you we were havin' spaghetti," said the first boy.

"I hope they don't run outta garlic bread," said the second boy.

One of the other girls broke in, "They always run outta bread by the end of the line."

"They do not!" said Todd pausing to look at the girl.

"Well, they might. And the bread's the best part," lamented the girl.

"Chill, Sara. If they run out you can have mine, okay?" Todd offered.

Todd Dillow led his charges into the cafeteria and after everyone was served and seated, got in line for his own dinner.

"What, no bread?" Todd asked a pleasant looking woman in her late fifties behind the steam table.

"Sorry, you're the last one. What took you so long?" asked the woman.

"Never mind," answered Todd as he slid his tray along and picked up a tall glass of tea.

"Dillow!" called a woman's voice from behind him.

He turned and saw Kathy Hopkins. Kathy was a student from the University of Nebraska he had met at last year's camp. They had become fast friends and even though their relationship stood on the very threshold of romance, they always addressed each other by their last names. She was a beautiful girl, in a natural, rustic sort of way: the type Todd always seemed to go for. She had large, deep, almond shaped brown eyes, and silky dark brown hair cut chin length. She wore a white tee shirt with a colorful logo from a radio station printed across the front, and a tan pair of shorts. *She looked great in shorts!*

"You got a package in the mail," said Kathy, holding a fairly large rectangle, wrapped in brown paper, "...*from England.*"

He looked at the package. *"England?"* asked Todd. *"Marion!"* thought Todd. He took the package from Kathy and instantly recognized Marion's handwriting.

"Who ya know in England?" asked Kathy.

"Uh... it's from a friend of mine I went to school with... and used to work with. You remember me telling you about the mad scientist?"

"Yeah. The one who made you do all those creepy experiments."

"Mm huh, that's the one. Marion...uh, that's her name... used to work at the lab too. She and Dr. Little had sort of a thing going."

Kathy raised her eyebrows and smiled naughtily.

"...Anyway," Todd went on, "...he got a professorship at the *Cambridge School of Internal Medicine* and fixed things up for her to go there next fall. They left right after school finished."

"Cambridge. Wow!"

"Yeah, tell me about it."

*****

It was very nearly midnight before Todd had a chance to open the package Marion had sent him. It was on his mind the whole evening, but his responsibilities allowed him no free time till everyone was in bed and asleep. The latter part, *asleep,* was always much later than the former part, *in bed.* Afterwards there was also the informal counselor meeting, where everyone was free to smoke a cigarette, sneak a beer, and to *cuss.*

Todd sat in a wooden rocking chair next to his bed in the quiet cabin and opened the package. Inside were a large notebook and a long letter written in Marion's hand. The letter read:

"Dear Todd,

I hope this letter gets to you before you read about what I've done in the papers. If this letter does not precede the media, I hope it will explain why I did what I was forced to do. If you haven't, or do not hear about what I am speaking of, chances are I was arrested or <u>killed</u> in the attempt, and was unsuccessful. If this was the case, I'm sorry, but I must pass this burden on to you. It is a terrible burden, but it is too important to let go unresolved, and by doing so would also make the sacrifice of my life be in vain. It boils down to the harsh reality of trading one life for a <u>billion</u>. If I have failed, you are possibly the only other person in the world who could, or would succeed me.

You know as much about Noah's viral strain as I do. You also know that if it got loose it would be a disaster unparalleled in all of history. Enclosed you will find Noah's journal. Please, read it carefully and make your own decision, then afterwards, dispose of it as per the instructions I have written in the back.

In giving you a condensed version, let me begin by saying he may be right and I might be in the wrong, and ultimately would be responsible for the end of the world. Which one of us is right? That is a decision you must reach for yourself, for what I am asking of you can only be undertaken with the most serious conviction and commitment. But in my heart, I know he is wrong, and have become convinced of this to the point that I am willing to give my life to stop him. Wisdom is not always the same thing as knowledge, and in the end it has always been the heart which is the seat of wisdom, rather than the mind.

What I am about to explain to you to say the least is a complex issue, so, let me attempt to start at the beginning. Noah Little believes that mankind has evolved to a plane where it is operating outside its natural parameters.

Modern medicine is keeping people alive too long, and modern warfare has advanced to the point large scale wars are not possible without annihilating both sides. Therefore, there will be no more large wars, and through improved medical care fewer and fewer people will succumb to terminal illness, and the average lifespan will grow longer and longer. He thinks because of this that populations will grow larger and faster than the earth's ability to support.

Noah blames the quote, 'lower classes,' of being the instigators of the population explosion. He goes on further to say they are breeding generations of emotionally disturbed offspring who are slowly destroying civilization. He also claims that these people are slowly devolutionizing the human species through the proliferation of defective genes. Noah believes that as a result of all these factors in approximately 135 years, society will break down, and all the people who are left will become something like prehistoric cavemen.

*So, Noah took it upon himself to alter the destiny he saw for the human race by coming up with a plan to weed out the majority of the earth's population that he saw as its nemesis from the segment he thought deserved to live. We were a part of that plan. You and I were actually helping him with a project called **'Weed Killer,'** not leukemia research.*

*Noah had everyone fooled for a long time, but the university trustees decided that he wasn't making any progress on the leukemia research he was supposedly doing, and pulled his grant. That's why he moved the lab to Cambridge where he has snowed the powers-that-be with the same shell and pea game. The virus Noah had us working on is like a **human insecticide.** He plans to contaminate large quantities of heroin with the Weed Killer virus and infect inner-city heroin addicts with the disease, and they will in turn pass it on to prostitutes, who* *will spread it to even wider numbers of his target segment.*

He figures that once the disease is set loose, millions of people would be infected and would start dropping like flies before the medical community had even a clue as to what they were dealing with. By then it would be too late. Educated people would become aware of the danger and would take proper precautions; and as most don't use heroin; and are more responsible with their procreation habits, would be in a lower risk group anyway. Therefore, Noah believes the majority of this segment would survive the plague, while his target segment would perish.

He thinks by doing this only people with superior social skills and intelligence would be left alive, thus cutting the crime rate to a fraction of the present figure increasing the average standard of living for the individual, and cleaning up the gene pool.

Noah believes that the majority of crime is drug related. By eradicating his target segment, the majority of crime would be eradicated as well; __fewer addicts - less drug related crime.__ If there are fewer people in the world, there would be less competition for its resources, so, it would follow that the overall individual living standard would improve. Also, he believes that the majority of society which does not pull its weight is within his target segment. By eliminating the target segment, the welfare state would be destroyed, and thus the burden would fall from those who are forced to finance it. And lastly, he believes that the lowest mentalities of the world's populations are within his target segment. Once they are gone, the average intelligence would be much higher, and their superior genetic makeup would proliferate a world of more enlightened people.

You and I mainly worked on the phase of the project that developed the virus. But towards the end we worked on a process of preserving it in a liquid medium that would keep the virus alive for months provided it was not exposed to temperatures less than zero Celsius. This was good enough to store mutated cultures in the laboratory, but the project required a step further.

The main objective of the Cambridge operation was to perfect a process that would place the virus in a suspended animation, and then trap it within a sugar crystal. Once this process was perfected the virus could remain in stasis indefinitely. Then the plan was to mix these stasis crystals with heroin. Given the potency of the virus, such small amounts could be mixed in that it would be virtually undetectable.

*Once the addict injected the heroin into his blood stream the sugar would be metabolized. The sugar crystals would melt freeing the virus, and then the blood's own oxygenation process would revive the virus from stasis. Once the virus was revived and in the blood stream, it would multiply - **and the rest you already know.***

Noah reckoned from hepatitis studies that addicts would in addition to sexual transmission; pass on the virus by sharing needles. He also figured that even after the disease was common knowledge, heroin is so strongly addictive, that addicts could not stop themselves, even knowing the risks, and would continue to transmit the disease right up to the end.

Noah claims that his target segment historically has demonstrated very little or no self-control, and would also be unable to abstain from unprotected sex. So, again the target segment would be unable to stop its own destruction because of its own inherent weakness.

As far as implementing the plan, he has that figured out too. He already has made several underworld connections, and has negotiated the purchase of 5 million dollars worth of pure heroin pending the perfection of the stasis crystals. Once he has contaminated the heroin, he plans to sell it for mere cents on the dollar! Noah Little would be left almost penniless, but the world heroin market would be glutted with virus-infected smack, and over a billion people would be dead in less than fifty years.

On the flip side of all this, I don't think Noah is right about this surgical precision he seems to think is going to take place in the eradication of his target segment. It's not going to be the clean, precise, incisions he believes. There is going to be an incredible amount of bleed-over between all the segments of the populace.

For example, drug abuse knows no social or economic boundaries. There are addicts in all walks of life. You can't say if you eliminate certain groups of people the problem will go away.

*Another point to consider is that I would dare say a lot of his target segment periodically sells pints of their blood to blood banks. When this occurs, hemophiliacs, people involved in traffic accidents, or anyone having serious operations would be at terrible risk. People in non-targeted segments have sex like anyone else, and would spread the disease the same way as the targeted segment. **And who is to say it will ever stop.** I think that it is a very real possibility that if Noah's virus gets loose it will eventually get us all.*

And all this empirical data he has gathered; as impressive as it may seem none of it has been corroborated by an outside study. He is one man working alone. There could be many factors he missed that could completely destroy the apparent accuracy of his conclusions.

Another thing which Noah omits is the survival instinct of the human species. Of all the creatures on the earth, man has always proved it's most adaptable. In one hundred and thirty five years people might be building cities on the moon, or harvesting giant farms on the bottom of the ocean. I refuse to accept Noah's gloom and doom prediction of an apathetic Armageddon. The human race will not just stick up its feet and roll over dead, it will go out kicking and screaming and hanging on for dear life like it has always done by its very nature.

And if Noah Little is right, and the human race is really destined to fade out of existence, **_let it be with honor._** I think it would be far better to be destroyed as a result of our compassion for one another, than to live because of our selfishness and prejudice.

Lastly, who is Noah Little that he should decide the fate of almost a third of the earth's population. For that matter, is there any mortal equipped for such a decision? I say no, and least of all Noah Little. These are matters best left for the Almighty God.

I know it seems impossible to believe that one man could wield such terrible power. But as you read his journal you'll see the diabolical genius of the man. He can and <u>will</u> pull it off if something is not done. He is just as committed to his philosophy as I am to my own. He believes he is acting nobly for the salvation of the human race, and is just as committed to following through with his plan as I am to stopping him.

I can't go to the police, for as of yet, he hasn't broken the law. And who would believe the story I just told you? I can hardly imagine such a thing myself, let alone convince someone who was not directly involved.

He's not some evil foreign government with large armies behind him - **_he is one man._**

It is mind boggling to think that a single person could hold such destructive power over so many.

That's the truly diabolical aspect of the whole scheme. No one could fathom a solitary individual would have the power to do what he WILL do, if not stopped. That is his greatest strength, but ironically, it is also his *greatest weakness. **What if Noah Little were dead?***

*As I write these words to you I stand in the wreckage of his laboratory. I have destroyed everything which could be used to duplicate this hellish thing... **but him.** Tonight, I will do everything in my power to kill Noah Little, and may God have mercy on my soul.*

I don't know if I can murder someone, but the lives of over a billion people are depending on me. If I fail, the Holocaust will pale by what Noah Little will bring into this world. If on the day you read this Noah Little still lives, it becomes your responsibility to stop him, as you are the only one capable of understanding or believing this letter, and taking the necessary action.

*Todd, you and I have never talked about the metaphysical. As a scientist, I never really thought that such things existed. Good and evil: I thought were just opposing perceptions of reality. If I have learned anything at all by all of this, it is that we are all a part of a great cosmic chess game, and there truly is a devil. Some of us are kings, queens, knights, and bishops; ...**some of us are pawns**. And it's possible for a pawn to win the game, provided it's on the right place on the board at the right time. And sometimes a pawn must be sacrificed to win the game - **sometimes two**.*

With all my love,

Mary "

CHAPTER SEVENTEEN

The rapid-fire notes of a harpsichord spat out of the stereo speakers in Noah Little's study, amidst the mellow, melodious accompaniment of a string quintet, as the recorded ensemble rendered selections from *Bach's Brandenburg Concertos.* Noah reclined in a large comfortable chair, listening blissfully, as he drained the last drops from *his fifth scotch.*

With a little difficulty he rose to his feet and walked over to the tape player and turned it off, plunging the empty residence into silence. He weaved a little as he walked.

Click-a-dee-clack-rattle-rattle. The strange sound came from the dark recesses of the unlighted hallway. Noah cocked an ear to listen. *Had he heard something?* He strained to listen again. *Nothing.* It must have been his imagination. He turned off the lamp in the study and headed down the hall for the stairs. He had barely made two steps up the staircase when he heard: *Clack-a-dee-click-rattle-rattle-clack.*

He was sure he heard something that time, and cautiously made his way into the kitchen. He turned on the lights. When the florescent tubes flickered on he saw nothing out of the ordinary, and heard only the low hum of the light tubes. *"It must be the air conditioner. Yes, that's it, just something wrong with the central air,"* he thought.

He went upstairs and prepared for bed. As he turned the covers down he heard the sound again, this time just outside the bedroom door. *Rattle-click-clack-dee-click-click.* Noah dashed out into the hall in search of the mysterious noise. He found nothing but the empty corridor.

He went back into the bedroom, turned out the lights, and went to bed. As he lay in the netherworld of awake and being almost asleep, he was suddenly brought back by the sound *Clack-a-click-rattle-rattle-clack-a-dee-clack.*

Noah stared in the direction of the noise. *CLICK!*

The lamp atop the chest of drawers popped on. A bony claw removed itself from the switch. Noah gazed in horror at the aberration to which the claw had belonged. There in the middle of his bedroom stood a human skeleton!

Clack-a-dee-click-rattle-rattle, was the sound it made as it walked across the room under its own power.

The skeleton was completely fleshless, except the eye holes of the hideous skull were filled with very animated human eyes. Noah had seen those eyes before. They were the eyes he had seen staring at him as they had sank into the acid tank. *They were Marion's.*

It stood beside his bed and looked at him. It spoke in Marion's voice, *"Let's get it on, stud."* Then it leaped on top of Noah with a loud thunderous clatter and ripped off his pajama top, then sank its bony digits into Noah's bare chest leaving ten long, scarlet, bleeding, scratches running from his pecs to his belly.

Noah screamed in pain and terror as he wriggled free of the skeleton, and then inched his way around the room, keeping his back to the wall. The skeleton rolled onto its back and followed him with its horrible eyes. When he had made his way to the wall opposite the foot of the bed, the skeleton slid its feet back, folding the legs, raising the knees high, then spread its legs wide, and rhythmically thrust its bony pelvis up and down in a mocking gesture of seduction.

"What's a matter Noah? Don't you want to *jump my bones?"* the skeleton asked sardonically.

Noah ran for the door. Behind him he heard a noisy rattling clatter. When he had almost reached the door the clattering commotion caught up with him, seized him by the shoulders and spun him around. Then the skull slowly moved up into his face and bit his lower lip. Noah screamed and spit blood upon the rib cage of the skeleton.

"Ah, that's what I always liked about you Noah, - *you're a great kisser,"* said the skeleton, and then abruptly slammed Noah into the wall with such awesome force that he made an indention into the sheetrock.

Noah started to crumple to the floor but the skeleton stopped him by slamming him back up against the wall again.

"What's a matter honey, *can't you get it up?* Here, let me help you." Saying that, it seized Noah's testicles with its right hand in a viselike grip. Noah howled in agony. The skeleton squeezed even tighter, sinking its sharp fingers into his scrotum till it oozed blood. Noah was screaming continuously now. Then it released its grip, and picked Noah up off the floor and held him aloft as if he were as light as a balloon. In a supernatural feat of strength, it threw him across the room, bouncing him off the ceiling, and back onto the bed.

Noah lay face down for a moment, and then slowly turned his face to the demon. The wind had been knocked from him; sharp spasms of pain stabbed him with each agonizing effort to breathe; some of his ribs were broken. The wounds from his lip and shirtless torso ran blood.

Clack-a-dee-clack-rattle-rattle-click-click. The clattering specter walked toward him. When it got near Noah's prone figure, it turned around and shoved its ugly rectum into Noah's face, then shook it violently back and forth like a hula dancer making a sickening rattle. It stopped, and looked over its bony shoulder with those terrible eyes.

"I guess my ass is not too fat for you now, is it?" asked the skeleton, then grabbed Noah by the shoulders again and savagely flipped him over onto his back. The

crotch of his pajama bottoms had been made crimson by his bleeding groin. His head slammed against the headboard of the bed, adding yet another instrument to his symphony of agony.

The skeleton slowly crawled into the bed with Noah, and pulled his pajama bottoms down to around his knees. The skeleton looked into Noah's horror filled eyes and said matter-of-factly, "You know what makes me such a good lover? ...*I give GREAT head!*" Then the skeleton laughed wildly.

Noah's eyes became as wide as saucers, and he managed to take in enough air to scream, "Noooooooooooo!"

The skeleton was on its knees straddling Noah's shins. It threw its head back and laughed even harder.

Then it stopped abruptly and looked down at Noah with dreadful malice. The skull's jaw opened mechanically, and then the skeleton went down on Noah. Cold, bony fingers guided Noah's penis into its hideous maul then... *CHOMP!*

*****

The half empty glass of scotch crashed to the floor shattering into a hundred pieces, the *Bach* played on majestically from the stereo speakers, and the phone rang furiously. Noah gasped and bolted upright in his chair, breathing laboriously as his heart pounded in his ears like a drum. He took in his surroundings and let out a long sigh of relief, then got up and turned off the music. The phone kept on ringing undaunted.

Noah answered the phone shakily, "Hello."

The voice at the other end was silent for a few beats, then asked, "Dr. Little?"

"Yes," answered Noah, "...Who is this?"

"It's Todd Dillow, Dr. Little."

"...Oh, Mr. Dillow."

"I was wondering, sir, if I could speak with Marion?"

There was a long pause as Noah gathered his thoughts.

"Marion Grand doesn't live here anymore. She left about three weeks ago."

This time it was Todd who paused for silent contemplation.

"...Do you know where she went, sir?"

"No, I don't. I'm afraid we had a bit of a falling out. I wouldn't trouble myself about it though. I'm sure she's fine. I expect she's off somewhere sight seeing; probably touring Europe and having a high ole time.

She'll most likely show up begging forgiveness a couple of weeks before classes start. That was the reason for our disagreement; she wanted to vacation and I wouldn't allow it. We simply had too much work to afford such an extravagance."

"...Oh, I see. Dr. Little, if you should hear from her, could you have her contact me? She knows how to reach me."

"Of course. Mr. Dillow, it was good hearing from you, but it's rather late, and this is not a good time. If you will excuse me, I really must go."

"Yes sir, I'm sorry to have disturbed you."

"That's quite all right. Perhaps we can speak again at length sometime in the near future. Good-bye, Mr. Dillow."

CHAPTER EIGHTEEN

On the other side of the planet, Todd Dillow hung up the pay phone outside the camp cafeteria. He had hardly slept a wink the night before, and had picked at his breakfast that morning. *"He sure sounded nervous; almost frightened,"* thought Todd, recalling the timbre of Noah's voice from the phone conversation they had just finished. Dr. Little's phrases were grouped in the usual cordial formality Todd had remembered, but there was something between the lines. At any rate, the man may have sounded nervous, *but he certainly didn't sound dead.*

Obviously, Marion had not killed Dr. Little, *but what had happened?* Had she lost her nerve, then run off to tour Europe like Little had suggested? Maybe she had changed her mind, or perhaps she hadn't, and was just off somewhere trying to summon up the courage to finally go through with it.

If the latter was the case, *should he warn Dr. Little?* Marion sounded pretty serious in the letter. Maybe, if he warned Little, he would take steps which would prevent her from carrying out her plan - thus saving his life, *and her future.* Todd found the image of Marion Grand spending a lifetime in prison almost unbearable. On the other hand, if he told Little, *what if he had her arrested?* The issue was brought down to the lesser of two evils: she would stand a far better chance of bouncing back from conspiracy to commit murder, than a bona fide, full fledged murder charge.

But what if she was right? He knew the nature of the work they had done in Little's laboratory, and he had known the good doctor to look down on certain groups of people with an awful loathing. The more he thought about it, the less farfetched it sounded. Indeed, *what if Marion Grand really was right?* Todd shuddered at the possibility.

Her letter conveyed a person reconciled and committed to a purpose, and his own knowledge of the woman told him she was not the type to go off half-cocked or make idle threats. And he had never known her not to follow through with something once she had begun, especially something for which she apparently had such a zealous passion.

But where was she? Had she attempted to kill Dr. Little and failed? If she had, and Little had foiled her attempt, why would he go through with such a charade over the phone? He remembered the lines in her letter: *"...I hope this will explain why I did what I was forced to do. If you haven't, or do not hear about what I am speaking of, chances are I was arrested or KILLED in the attempt ..."*

She could have tried to kill him and he could have turned the tables on her. *Would Dr. Little kill someone?* If Marion's letter was to be believed; *yes*.

If he had killed her, and Little was out to exterminate over a billion people with a real, workable, plan that he could actually implement independently through his own resources, what should he: Todd Dillow, do about it? *What could he do about it?* Was he now morally bound to finish what Marion Grand had started, and if Noah Little had actually done away with her, *avenge her death?* Was he now called by fate to kill Dr. Little? *Could he really murder someone? Could he walk away from it knowing what he knew?* He began to imagine the hell Marion must have went through. She undoubtedly wrestled with the same questions and moral dilemmas.

Over a three day span these thoughts and more consumed Todd, as he read with horror the words of Noah's journal. A profound depression took him as their intent became clearer. More and more he began to share Marion's appraisal of the journal's meaning, and the inclination and ability of Dr. Little to carry out the scheme described therein.

*****

"What cha readin', Dillow," asked Kathy Hopkins from the gloom of the moonlight.

Todd sat in a metal folding chair on the porch of his cabin, reading the last of the journal by the light of an overhead fixture. Kathy was silhouetted slightly in the shadows, but he could make out the details of her smiling face and lithe figure. She was dressed almost like a harlequin: black sweat pants and a white long sleeve sweatshirt, as it was rather chilly at the mountain retreat after sunset.

Todd closed the book, exhaled, shook his head, and said sadly, *"The Diary of a Madman."*

"Whew! Sounds like a hellva bedtime story. Think I could tear you away from the macabre for a minute?"

"Sure, what's up?"

"It's Sara. I can't get her to go to sleep. She's having nightmares again. She's kinda sweet on you and I thought if you could come down and talk to her... well ...maybe?" Kathy explained with a shrug.

Todd slowly smiled. "Hopkins? Just what would all of you helpless women do without Todd Dillow?"

"Well, I guess that just proves without a doubt that *love is blind.*"

"Hopkins! That's ... *that's sick.*"

"I'm sorry, it just sorta slipped out," Kathy said amidst embarrassed giggles.

Todd stepped half inside his cabin, and tossed the journal onto his bed, then exited letting the noisy door spring slam the screen door closed. He joined the woman and put his arm around her shoulder, and then the couple started down the steep hill.

147

"Next thing I know you'll be tellin' *Helen Keller jokes*," said Todd in exasperation.

Kathy responded by elbowing him in the ribs, then draping her arm around his waist.

"Ouch!"

*****

Sara was crying softly when Kathy and Todd entered the little dormitory. There were three other girls who shared the room with her, two were asleep, and the third was kneeling near the bed trying to comfort the little girl.

Todd put his hand on the shoulder of the kneeling girl and whispered in her ear, "All right Tiffy, go back to bed, now," then guided her to Kathy, who led her to her bed and tucked her in.

"Hey, hey, what's all this about?" asked Todd sitting on the edge of the bed next to the crying girl, and then wiped the tears from her cheeks.

Sara was a rather comely child, ten years old, with long coarse brown hair and freckles, but usually exhibited the most vivacious of personalities.

She sat up in her bed and hugged Todd tightly and started to cry even harder.

"Shush, shush, it's all right. Shush," he whispered as he held her in his arms and rocked gently back and forth.

When the little girl had calmed down, he laid her back down in her bed, and put his hand on her belly.

"Did you have a bad dream?"

"Uh huh."

"You know bad dreams aren't real. They can't hurt us, ya know."

"But it was so scary."

"Uh huh. You wanna talk about it?"

Sara spoke quickly, running her sentences together, and she started to cry again. "...I dreamed I woke up and everybody in the world was gone, and I kept callin' and nobody would answer me. I went outside and I got lost and I kept runnin' into bushes. Then there was bushes all around me and I couldn't get out. I was cryin' but nobody would help me 'cause I was the only person in the world and I was alone."

"It's all right. It's all right. Shush, shush," Todd said reassuringly. "I'm right here, and so is Kathy, and Tiffy, and Georgia, and Mandy, and next Friday is parent's day, and your mom and dad will be here. And there's people all over the world, millions and millions and... *billions* ...of people, you're not alone. Okay?"

Sara said nothing.

"Okay?" Todd repeated, and then started to tickle her under the chin.

Sara started to giggle and held her chin down on her chest. Then Todd tickled her under the armpit.

"Okay? Okay? ...Okay?" asked Todd, tickling the child.

"Okay!" answered Sara, as she tried to hold the volume of her laughter.

"Well, all right! That's my girl." said Todd. He looked at the child and smiled. "Now, you get some sleep, okay?"

"Okay, Todd."

"Yeah?"

"Uh huh."

"You better."

"I will."

"And no more bad dreams."

"No more bad dreams."

"That's my girl," said Todd, then bent down and kissed her on the cheek. "Good night, Sara."

"Good night, Todd."

"Good night, Sara," whispered Kathy Hopkins' voice from the doorway.

"Good night, Kathy," answered Sara.

Dillow and Hopkins walked silently from the cabin holding hands in the moonlight. When they had gotten out of earshot of the cabin, Hopkins commented, "Not bad, Dillow, not bad."

"All in a day's work, my lady," came Dillow's response.

"You're really good with kids," she said admiringly.

"Sara's a cute kid."

"Yeah, but I think you handled that rather well."

"Thanks."

The couple walked on in silence till they found themselves in front of a small pond. There were twelve rows of wooden benches erected at the pond's shore the camp used for outdoor vesper services. They sat down on one of the benches, and Kathy put her head on Todd's shoulder as they took in the scene.

Moonlight danced on the water, shimmering from time to time when the gentle breeze disturbed the surface of the pond. A chorus of crickets chirped as a lone bullfrog bellowed in a low throng from the other side of the pond.

"Hopkins?"

"Mmm?"

"Do you think Sara has much of a life?"

Kathy sat up to look at Todd's face. It was pained, and deadly serious. "What do you mean?" she asked.

Todd thought for a moment. "...I mean, the girl is blind. She's never seen the stars, or the moon. She's never seen a sunset..." He paused to look deep into Kathy's eyes, and then went on, "...She's never seen a pretty face... or a flower, or the ocean, or the sky, or the mountains... *and she never will.*"

They pondered for a moment, then Todd said, "And she was born that way. It's congenital. One day her children might be blind too."

"You don't know that," Kathy protested.

"It's a possibility. Aside from that, right now; *what kind of life has she?* Think of all the things she's missing. And she's such a good kid too. It's just not fair. There's murderers, rapists, and criminals of all sorts out there: truly evil people with two good eyes, and that... that beautiful soul down there is sentenced to 70 more years of darkness. What did she do to deserve that? NOTHING!

What kind of life does she have? If she has to live the rest of it like that, wouldn't she really be better off dead? ...Or never even born to begin with?"

Kathy was silent for a long while, then scooted away from Todd on the bench a bit and took both of his hands in hers.

"Close your eyes," she commanded firmly.

Todd did as he was told.

"*Now, listen,*" she said, and the two sat nearly motionless almost ten minutes.

Todd heard the crickets and the frog. He felt the breeze upon his face. Something jumped in the water and the ripples echoed slowly away. He could smell Kathy's perfume. It smelled sweet and pleasant. He realized that he hadn't noticed it at all before.

Kathy took his hands and touched them to her face, then to her lips, and to her hair. Her hair felt soft and silky. Then she kissed him on the lips. Her kiss was moist and gentle. She spoke: her voice sounding almost like music.

"If from this point on you could never open your eyes again... *would your life be worth living?*"

His eyes sprang open to behold her lovely face inches from his. All the sadness he had felt since Marion had left hit him all at once, but all his doubt and indecision lifted from him in the same instant. There were no more questions. *He had an answer now.*

"Yes," said he, then broke down and began to weep. Kathy held him in her arms, and soon silent tears ran down her cheeks as well.

*****

Todd Dillow looked rather conspicuous as he entered the *First National Bank* wearing his camping garb. He walked up to the teller holding the pass book to his bank account. The small book represented all the funds he had accumulated to pay for his first year of medical school.

He handed the pass book to the teller and said, "I'd like to make a withdrawal".

The teller took the book and read the name of its owner. "How much do you wish to withdraw, Mr. Dillow?" asked the teller cheerfully.

Todd swallowed hard, and then said, *"All of it."*

CHAPTER NINETEEN

"...Be sure and get receipts for everything, and please have them open the boxes and examine the beakers and test tubes. I don't intend to pay for broken glass. Is that understood?" asked Noah scowling.

"Yes, sir," answered Patti Meeks.

Noah retrieved a lab coat from a hook at the end of the cage room. He slipped into the coat, wincing a little from the pain in his sore shoulder, then reached into his pants pocket and produced the keys to his BMW. He handed the keys to her and warned, "Be careful with the car."

"I will."

"All right, off with you, now."

"Okay, I'll see you later."

Noah responded by turning his back, picking up a clipboard off a desk near to where he was standing and flipping through its pages.

Patti looked at him awkwardly, and then left silently.

"Where's the bloody ape?" asked Dr. Kirby-Smythe, appearing seemingly from thin air.

Noah whirled around to find the tall, lanky scientist looking about the cages for Cheetah. *"Damn! I've got to remember to start keeping that door locked,"* thought Noah.

"Oh, Dr. Kirby-Smythe, good afternoon," Noah said, trying to hide his irritation.

Kirby-Smythe nodded curtly, and then repeated his question, "Ya ape; where's ya ape?"

"The chimpanzee; oh, yes. I'm afraid he died in an experiment," answered Noah coldly.

Kirby-Smythe's features expressed a touch of regret. "Ah for shame; the little bugger had right spirit, he did. A pity it is to be sure." His face remained dark for a moment, then suddenly brightened. "I see ya got a new assistant, and a lovely girl she is to boot. Now, what be her name?"

"...Patti Meeks."

"Patti Meeks, you say. What become of Miss Grand?"

"Well, Dr. Kirby-Smythe," began Noah as he thrust his hands into the pockets of his lab coat, "...Miss Grand and I had a parting of the ways on a few things."

Noah stopped speaking abruptly. Something was in the right pocket of his coat. He pulled out a loaded syringe. It was the viral injection he had been preparing to give Cheetah just before he left for the weekend at Kirby-Smythe's.

"Sorry to hear that, I am, Dr. Little. I was beginnin' to take to the girl, I was," lamented Kirby-Smythe.

Noah's eyes widened when he beheld the small plastic hypodermic as if he were looking at the *Holy Grail.*

"Did ya Miss Grand take back to the states?" asked Kirby-Smythe.

"This is wonderful!" thought Noah. Now, all he had to do was empty the syringe's contents into a growth medium, put it in an incubator, sit back, and let it multiply. He would not have to go through the long tedious process of mutating the hoof and mouth virus again. He'd be back on schedule in less than a month!

"Well, did she?"

Noah was so absorbed in his discovery he hadn't noticed Kirby-Smythe was speaking.

"What? I'm ...I'm sorry Dr. Kirby-Smythe, What, what did you say?" Noah asked.

Kirby-Smythe regarded Noah strangely, and then repeated his question, "I said did Miss Grand return to the United States?"

"I'm not sure. I would imagine. She left in the night and didn't confide her plans to me," answered Noah hesitantly.

Kirby-Smythe noticed the way Noah was staring at the syringe in his right hand and the surprised look on his face since he had pulled it from his pocket.

"That be something important ya found in ya pocket just now?" he asked.

Noah looked uncomfortable with the question. He quickly pocketed the syringe and shook his head saying, "No, nothing important."

"Cryin' shame, it is. I mean about Miss Grand, that is. Just popping off like that," said Kirby-Smythe changing back to his original topic.

"Yes, it is. Miss Grand was a woman of many attributes and assets. I will miss her greatly," Noah said reflectively, as remorse began to tug at his heart's strings.

Just then the phone rang in the outer lab. He walked to the desk, then picked up the extension and answered, "Little." His expression showed great astonishment. "What? ...Ah huh... Yeah, that's mine... Ah huh... (long pause) ...She works for me... Be right down."

Noah hung up the phone and faced his bewildered visitor. "Dr. Kirby-Smythe, do you think you might be so kind as to give me a ride to *Mercy Hospital?"*

"...Why certainly. What's da matter?" questioned Kirby-Smythe with concerned.

Noah looked grave. "It seems that my assistant, Patti Meeks... *has been involved in a rather serious traffic accident."*

*****

The next day Noah was in his office early via a rented car. His own car was a total loss, and Patti Meeks was not a great deal better off than the car. He would have to find another assistant, for he was sure her convalescence would be a lengthy one. He had just sat down at his desk when there was a knock on the open door of his office.

The visitor was a rather portly man with red hair and freckles about fifty years of age. He wore black horn rimmed glasses, a rumpled suit, and a shirt which was much too tight for the belly it covered.

"Dr. Little, Dr. Noah Little?" asked the man.

Noah looked up from his desk. "Yes," said he, as he removed his glasses and set them down on the document he had been perusing.

"I'm Inspector Flaherty of the Cambridge Police Department. Could I trouble you for a short interview, sir? ... About yesterday's accident."

Noah looked at the policeman stone-faced, and then motioned to a chair in front of his desk. Flaherty withdrew a notebook from his inside coat pocket and sat down.

He opened the small notepad and began, "Thank you, Dr. Little. I promise to take only a few moments of your time. Now then, Miss uh ..., " the inspector consulted the pad for the name, "...Miss ...Patti Meeks is a person of your employ?"

"Yes, she's my lab assistant and all around *Girl Friday*," Noah answered.

"I see, and it is a habit of yours to allow her the use of your vehicle?"

"On occasion; when it's in the routine of business."

"Mm hum. But this is not something you do on a day to day basis?"

156

"No."

Flaherty made a note in his pad. "Do you know if Miss Meeks had any enemies; any jilted boyfriends, etc.?"

Noah looked confused. "No. I haven't known Miss Meeks very long, and it has not been our practice to discuss our personal lives."

"I see. How about you? Dr. Little, do you have any enemies?" the inspector asked, looking unblinkingly into Noah's eyes.

Noah glanced at the skeleton just behind Flaherty.

"Inspector, what is this all about?"

"I'm sorry to say, Dr. Little, but we are most certain there was foul play involved in yesterday's accident."

"Foul play?"

"Yes, sir, I'm afraid so."

"What... what do you mean?"

"The brake lines of your vehicle were deliberately cut. Miss Meeks left the parking lot of the university, turned down a steep hill, and ran broadside of four lanes of traffic. She had absolutely no control over the vehicle."

Noah's face turned rather pale.

"I do not wish to alarm you, Dr. Little," Flaherty went on, noticing Noah's worried countenance, "... but as a precaution I would like to assign you police protection for a couple of days. I assure you our men will be very inconspicuous, and in view of the situation, I'm sure you'll sleep the better for it."

"Yes, you're quite right. Thank you... I would appreciate it."

"Is there anyone you would be remotely unsure about?"

"...I'm sorry, I don't understand."

"...Anyone you may have had any sort of altercation with: a disgruntled student, perhaps. Anything would be helpful."

"...No, I can't think of anyone like that. This is my first year, and classes just started a week ago."

Flaherty rose, removed his wallet, and retrieved a business card, then handed it to Noah saying, "If you should think of anything, no matter how trivial, please feel free to call."

Noah took the card and examined it, then looked questioningly at the policeman.

Flaherty shook Noah's hand. "Good day, Dr. Little." he said in parting, then turned and left.

CHAPTER TWENTY

All that day Noah jumped at every sound. *Was someone trying to kill him?* If so, *who? Did Marion Grand have an accomplice?* When he finished his classes he went straight home. The last place he wanted to be was alone in his laboratory late at night.

When he pulled up into his driveway he noticed the unmarked police car. *At least he hoped it was the police and not the assassins.*

He took a long hot shower, prepared and ate his dinner, and *before, during, and after,* consumed a large amount of scotch whiskey. He kept the stereo blaring classical music at a deafening level the whole evening. When the house was silent, every sound represented an unseen villain lurking somewhere in the shadows. It was shortly after 2 AM when exhaustion began to overpower paranoia, and he finally went to bed.

*****

The sound of splashing water was the first thing he became aware of. He opened his eyes to find he was in a long gondola traversing a large fog laden body of still water.

The boat was made of polished ebony and adorned with gold trim. As visibility was only a few yards, he could not see where the boat was sailing, nor from where it had come. When he looked behind him he discovered in horror to find his gondolier was *Death:* a black robed, hooded skeleton. The hood obscured the skull, but two bony claws held the paddle as it rowed the boat smoothly along. *It spoke with Marion's voice.*

"Rather balmy tonight, don't you think, Noah?" asked *Death.*

Noah made no answer, but moved to the bow of the boat in terror.

The hooded figure laughed and said, *"Honey, don't you think this is kinda romantic?"*

"Why are you doing this to me?" Noah shrieked.

"Got somethin' to show you," sang *Death* in a spooky, taunting melody, then pointed a bony digit straight ahead.

Noah looked in the direction in which the specter had pointed. He heard the sound of a great multitude murmuring off in the distance. The sound grew louder as they approached. Slowly, the fog began to lift, and Noah saw the largest crowd of people he had ever seen assembled in one place. There were hundreds of thousands of them, *perhaps millions*. People lined the shore as far as he could see in both directions, and straight ahead on into the mountains. Someone was standing on every square foot of earth, except for a wooden dock that ran to a square platform elevated six feet or so above the crowd, and a hundred yards out into the multitude there was a two hundred foot circle cleared with a large pole in its center.

Death sprang gingerly from the boat and tied it to the dock. "Come on, Noah, *you're the guest of honor*," said the hooded ghost, and offered him a bony hand.

Noah considered the appendage, and then climbed onto the dock unassisted, while *Death* chuckled.

It led him to the edge of the platform, and the mass began to chant in an eerie whisper, *" Noah ...Noah ... Noah."*

"Behold, Noah Little: *your children,*" said the skeleton as it made a sweeping gesture to the enormous crowd with both hands.

"Noah ... Noah ... Noah ... Noah ... Noah ... Noah ... Noah ... Noah ..." the multitude whispered in unison.

Icy terror gripped Noah's heart when he noticed for the first time that the multitude was not a multitude of people, *but an enormous resurrected graveyard.* There were millions of animated corpses, all in varying degrees of decomposition and decay. Some were merely gray in paler, some had large chunks of their rotting flesh missing, some had eyes hanging from their gaping sockets, and some were just horrible walking skeletons, with no flesh at all clinging to their hideous frameworks.

"Behold, Noah Little: *your children,*" repeated *Death.*

Noah shrank away from the nightmarish vision. "Why do you call... *that...* my *children?"* he asked, barely audible over the chanting masses.

"Because Noah Little, those are the souls of all the people who will die from your virus: *a third of mankind,"* answered *Death,* then took hold of his shoulders with its talons, and whirled him around. Noah could see the skull clearly now in the recesses of the black hood with *Marion's eyes* staring at him accusingly; its hideous jaw working up and down as it spoke.

"You made them like this," *Death* went on, "... and all their unborn children." The hooded skeleton turned Noah back around and pushed him forward to the edge of the platform.

The huge crowd chanted louder and louder, "*Noah ... Noah ... Noah ... Noah ... Noah ...Noah ..."*

Death stood behind Noah's left shoulder and had to yell to be heard over the chanting, "Look at them, Noah Little! LOOK AT THEM! Behold your legacy!" Then *Death* laughed in a loud screeching wail.

"... Noah ... ... Noah ... Noah ... Noah ... Noah ... Noah ... Noah ... Noah," chanted the crowd.

Death switched to Noah's right, laying a bony hand upon his shoulder, and then asked, "Ever been to a rock concert, Professor?"

Noah was too terrified to respond.

"Ever heard of *stage divin'?*"

"Noah ... Noah ... Noah ... Noah! ... Noah! ... NOAH! ... NOAH! ... NOAH! ...NOAH! ... NOAH! ... NOAH! ... NOAH!"

"No? Well …let me introduce you to the sport. I'm sure you're really *gonna fall... in love with it,"* said *Death* deadpan, and then pushed Noah into the sea of moving corpses. **"Welcome to HELL, Dr. Little!"**

Noah fell head long into a sea of rotting hands. He could hear *Death's* maniacal laughter fading behind him as he was held aloft and passed forward over the heads of the multitude while their damnable chanting grew louder and faster. He kept his eyes tightly closed as to not see their hellish faces. Suddenly, he fell to the ground with a terrible jolt. He stood up to find himself in the clear circle, facing the large pole.

"NOAH! ... NOAH! ... NOAH! ... NOAH! ... NOAH!"

A platoon of cadavers emerged from the multitude carrying large pieces of dry wood, and began to pile them around the pole. The corpses around the perimeter of the circle could be heard cheering wildly over the rhythmic chanting of the enormous assemblage.

When the wood was piled five feet high around the pole, the leader of the platoon started toward Noah. It was a tall decaying corpse with no eyes, but a thin layer of leathery skin covering its skull. The jaw hung wide open and oddly disjointed, and swung back and forth with the movement of its large body.

Noah ran from it. He stopped at a wall of dead faces, which ceased chanting and hissed at him.

"NOAH! ... NOAH! ... NOAH! ...NOAH! ... NOAH!"

He ran to the other side of the circle. He slid to a stop in front of another hissing mob.

"NOAH! ... NOAH! ... NOAH! ... NOAH! ... NOAH!"

He turned and ran again, this time running straight into the arms of the leader of the cadaver platoon. It folded its arms around Noah in a bear hug, forcing his face into its rotting chest. The crowd cheered. *The smell was horrific.*

The next thing Noah knew he was tied to the pole and was smelling smoke. Soon flames were all around him. The heat was intense. He began to scream. He could hear the cheering crowd and the hellish, unending chant.

"NOAH! ... NOAH! ... NOAH! ... NOAH! ... NOAH!"

He looked down between the flames and saw Marion standing at the foot of the burning stake. But it wasn't the *Demon Marion,* it was the *Living Marion:* the beautiful young woman he remembered from happier times.

"Marion! Help me!" he screamed.

"NOAH! ... NOAH! ... NOAH! ... NOAH! ... NOAH!"

"Help me! Please Marion! Please help me!"

"NOAH! ... NOAH! ... NOAH! ... NOAH! ... NOAH!"

Marion looked at Noah and shook her head.

"Please Marion. HELP!"

Marion slowly walked up to the pile of burning wood, then straight into the fire. Her clothing instantly burst into flames. She didn't cry out or show any sign of pain; just slowly and methodically ascended the pile of burning wood then stopped two feet in front of the bound Noah Little.

Noah could smell the pungent fumes of her burning flesh. Her long flowing hair quickly turned into thin black threads, and her face blackened and lost its human form. Only the eyeballs remained, shining an unearthly white from the charcoaled face. The arms reached out and grabbed both of Noah's shoulders. He could feel the stiff fingers, and the papery skin falling away from them as the hands gripped his shoulders.

The fire began to burn his own body. He could feel searing agony in his legs, and began to scream. The mouth of Marion's incinerated face began to bend into an insipid smile.

*****

Noah coughed violently as the fireman rolled him from the bed and smothered out his burning pajamas with the bedspread.

"What's going on?" Noah wheezed.

"Try to stay calm, gov'na, the bloody house is on fire! But you're gonna be all right," exclaimed an English accent. Then suddenly, Noah was aware that he was being carried down a staircase. There was smoke everywhere and a loud roaring sound. There were many excited shouts from all parts of the house, and sirens outside.

The next thing he was aware of, he was on a stretcher with an oxygen mask over his face, being lifted into the back of an ambulance. The last thing he saw was the sight of his burning house framed by the open door of the ambulance. The door slammed shut... *then darkness.*

CHAPTER TWENTY-ONE

"Well, Dr. Little, it could have been a lot worse, *a whole lot worse*," reported Dr. Julian Anders. "... You've a few second degree burns on your legs and right forearm, but outside of that, and a little smoke inhalation, I'd say you weathered everything extremely well."

Noah sat up in the hospital bed slightly and thought of his throbbing calves.

"You had best stay the rest of the day and overnight. I'll probably discharge you in the morning if there are no unexpected complications. You should stay outta work for a day or two, and then you can resume your duties."

Noah looked the young doctor up and down: a tall handsome man with dark hair and an athletic build; just barely thirty-five.

"Impertinent young fool," thought Noah. *Who was he to tell him when he could go to work or not, or when he could leave the hospital?* Noah had been pulling emergency room shifts when this boy was waiting for his acne to clear up. Still, he had no home to go back to - just as well stay here as a hotel.

"Is there anything we could get for you to make your stay here with us more comfortable?" asked Anders politely.

Noah shook his head.

"Well, if there is nothing else, or if you haven't any questions, I'll take my leave of you, sir," said Anders, turning to go.

Noah nodded.

Anders walked half way across the small private hospital room and abruptly stopped, snapped his fingers, and turned to face Noah.

"There's a chap out in the waiting area from the police who would like to speak with you. Do you feel up to it?" asked the young doctor.

Noah thought for a moment then said, "That would be fine".

"All right, I'll send him right in. See you this afternoon."

Anders left, and about ten minutes later was replaced by the hulking form of Inspector Raymond Flaherty.

"I don't know what you call police protection in this country, but it is certainly different from what we'd call it in the *States*," reprimanded Noah with venom.

Flaherty cringed a little from the assault. The operative he had assigned to watch Noah's house had fallen asleep on the job. He had just finished chewing him out royally before leaving for the hospital. Now, it was his turn to get the *butt chewing*. He guessed he had this coming.

The inspector looked hotly embarrassed and began to apologize. "Let me begin, Dr. Little, by offering you my condolences for the loss of your home--"

"I thought you people were supposed to be watching the fuckin' house. Where were the police when that son of a bitch was sprinkling gasoline all over my living room? - ASLEEP?" interrupted Noah.

That stung Flaherty, however he would not admit to Little that that was indeed, exactly the way it had been. "You heard that it was arson, then?" asked Flaherty dolefully, trying not to lose his professionalism.

"No shit, Sherlock!"

"In my man's defense let me point out that he did save your life. Your home is in a remote area and would have surely burned to the ground unobserved, and you along with it, had he not summoned the fire department."

Noah softened a little.

Flaherty pulled out his ever present notepad and continued, "I'm happy to say that a great deal of your possessions were salvaged, and the house is repairable. Best of all, Constable Stokes caught the arsonist."

Noah brightened. "Are you saying you caught the bastard who torched my house?"

"Yes, sir; a viable suspect is in custody."

Noah sighed with satisfaction. "Well, I suppose that does knock a bit of the curse off it."

The rotund policeman ambled over and rolled his bulk into a chair opposite Noah's bed. He consulted his notepad and frowned. Looking into Noah's eyes, asked, "Do you know a gentleman by the name of *Todd Dillow?"*

"Todd Dillow?" repeated Noah in disbelief, as he sat up in the bed.

"You know him then?"

"What does *Todd Dillow* have to do with anything?"

"An overwhelming amount of evidence suggests that he set fire to your house, which casts a shadow of suspicion upon him as being connected with the incident involving your motorcar."

"Yeah, but... *Todd Dillow*?"

"I take it then you are acquainted with Mr. Dillow?"

"Yeah, he worked for me at my last posting back in America. He's just a kid ...*harmless*. I can't believe he would be capable of something like that. Besides, what's he doing here in England anyway?"

"He is of course, a very young man, but our preliminary investigations suggest that he is NOT *harmless.* In fact he is in great likelihood, guilty of two attempts on your life, sir. As for his residence in the United Kingdom? Apparently, he came here to murder you."

Flaherty closed his notepad, sat back in the chair, and stared at Noah with eyes that looked as if they could possibly pierce into his very soul. "What I would like to know is... *why?"*

CHAPTER TWENTY-TWO

Inspector Waverly shook his head, and looked from Todd Dillow to Raymond Flaherty and back to Dillow again.

"Son, you're in a lot of trouble. Best come clean with us now, and maybe things will run a little better for you in the end," advised Waverly.

Robert Waverly was a tall whip of a man with black hair and a pencil thin mustache. The three of them: Waverly, Flaherty, and Dillow had been in one of the Cambridge Police Department's interrogation rooms for just a little under two hours, and Todd had told them very little beyond his name and address.

"We've received telexes from authorities in the United States and have found that you have no criminal record. You're a pre-med student with good grades. The last job you had was at a *camp for blind kids,* for pity's sake. You seem hardly the type to burn down someone's house," remarked Flaherty incredulously.

"Why, Todd?" asked Waverly, "...Why did you do it?"

"Might it have something to do with this?" asked Flaherty, and shoved a file across the table at Todd.

Todd considered the file for a moment, then opened the folder and flipped through its pages wide-eyed. "Where did you get this?" Todd asked Flaherty.

"It was in with your possessions taken from your hotel room," answered Flaherty.

Todd looked at the ceiling and drew a long breath, then looked down at the open folder in front of him. *Inside was Marion's letter.*

"And you've read it?" Todd asked.

Flaherty nodded.

Todd looked questioningly at Waverly.

Waverly nodded.

"Shit!" Todd whispered, then said, "Well, fellas, there you have it," closed the file, and slid it back across the table to Flaherty.

"You believe that Dr. Little is going to kill a billion people with a virus?" asked Waverly.

"Yes," answered Dillow coldly.

"Mmm, I see," commented Waverly in a patronizing tone.

"You don't believe it, do you?" Todd asked Waverly.

Waverly said nothing.

"You think I'm nuts," Todd said, turning to Flaherty.

Flaherty said nothing.

"You weren't there. You didn't see the experiments. The way the animals died. That's why we had to take matters into our own hands. No one would have ever believed such a fantastic story. *But it's true,* and now that I've failed, we're all screwed."

Todd hung his head for a moment, and then was suddenly struck with an inspiration.

"Wait a minute. There's still a chance to stop the maniacal son of a bitch. You really don't have to believe me. *I think that Noah Little has killed Marion Grand.* I don't know how or what he did with the body, *but he killed her.* I've called all her friends and family I could think of, and no one's seen or heard from her. Dammit! Her own father has even got a missing person's trace out after her. Check on **that** and you will see that it's true.

You don't have to believe me. But what I've told you

raises enough doubt to put some suspicion on Dr. Little. It's enough to warrant you having a talk with him anyway... Well, doesn't it?"

"...Yes, I suppose so. But Dr. Little is not the issue here," said Waverly.

"Look! I set fire to the house. Give me some paper. I'll make a formal statement; just go out there and nail that bastard before he kills us all."

"And the motorcar?" asked Flaherty.

"Yep, I did that too. The son of a bitch has more lives than a fuckin' cat!" admitted Todd.

*****

When Noah Little was released from the hospital he checked into a hotel near the university where he haggled with insurance companies for about three days. He wanted to make a cash settlement and just start over in a new house. But the insurance company insisted on repairing his old one. After he capitulated to that course, he then seemed to be forever on the phone with contractors, painters and electricians. Knowing that it would be a very long time before his home would be made livable, he rented a flat.

In the midst of all these negotiations, the insurance company paid him for the BMW Patti Meeks had crashed, and he purchased a new car, this time a tan Mercedes. Patti Meeks had been moved out of intensive care. But it was as Noah had feared: she would not be able to resume her duties at the lab. Noah sandwiched in interviews for the vacant position between phone calls with insurance companies, contractors and his own busy teaching schedule. He found no one remotely suitable. It was just as well. He had no time to train a new assistant even if he could have found one. His Cambridge teaching responsibilities were extremely demanding, a lot more than he would have ever anticipated. There was absolutely no time to work on Weed Killer; a situation that left him in a constant state of being... *pissed!*

*****

"The bloke was tellin' the truth about that'en," said Robert Waverly, as he dropped the hard copy printout on Flaherty's desk.

Flaherty picked up the report and scanned it. It was a missing person report on one: *Marion Elizabeth Grand.* Waverly plopped down in the chair in front of Flaherty's desk.

"How do you like that?" asked Waverly.

Flaherty whistled.

"And that's not the half of it. Our boy was right about Dr. Little and Miss Marion shackin' up too."

"Bobby, how much of his story do you believe?"

"You mean all this business about a *doomsday germ?*"

"Mm huh."

"...I believe *he believes it.*"

"Can you imagine gettin' a spooky thing like that letter in the mail?"

"Yeah. It's little wonder the poor chap went off half cocked the way he did."

Flaherty's features turned somber. "Do you suppose there could be truth in any of the rest of his story?"

"Raymond! You can't be serious. Next you'll be tellin' me you believe in the *Bigfoot and the UFO's.*

It's more apt to be a lover's squabble. The girl has a

172

fight with the old doctor and makes up this whole cockamamie plot to get our man in there to bump him off. Then the sap thinks about all the lab rats they all killed together and falls for it hook line and sinker," explained Waverly.

"Still, I can't think of any reason not to have a chat with Dr. Little about Marion Grand," said Flaherty, furrowing his brow.

"Well, neither can I. But be careful. After the cluster fuck Stokes pulled, I don't think we oughta be pissin' around with a world renowned scientist whose house we just let burn down."

"This is true. I'll be subtle."

"Careful, the word is *careful*, Raymond. Little has already lodged a formal complaint with the old man. And you and I are much too old to be walkin' a beat. There's no need to be pourin' petrol on the flames, is there now?"

"I want you to come with me."

"Me?"

"I've met Little a time or two and there's just something that strikes me peculiar about the man. I want you to meet him and see what you think."

"I'll go, but I'll be keepin' a rein on you is what I'll be doin'. Please man; don't land us in the same boiling pot as Stokes."

CHAPTER TWENTY-THREE

"No, no, no! The policy says replacement cost...

Hell, I don't know, I didn't keep receipts for all of that! ...Look, the only thing I had left was my pajamas and the gown the hospital gave me - *not exactly the conservative garb worn by university professors..."* barked Noah into his telephone.

Flaherty and Waverly stood at the threshold of Noah Little's office. Noah looked up from behind his desk and noticed the two detectives, then motioned for them to enter.

"No! That will not be acceptable! ..." said Noah as his eyes narrowed.

There was only one other chair in the small office. Flaherty sat down while Waverly stood.

"I don't have time to go back to all the stores I've bought clothes from in the past week and get copies of the receipts. Why can't you do that? ...Well, what the hell did I pay all those damn premiums for? ..."

Noah was silent for a long while as the sound of a man's voice escaped from the phone's handset loudly enough for everyone in the room to hear. When Noah had heard enough, he slammed the receiver down making the phone ring slightly, and then glared wordlessly at Flaherty as if to say, *Now, what the hell do you want?*

Inspector Flaherty took his cue and began politely, "Dr. Little, this is my associate, Inspector Waverly," and motioned to the standing policeman to his left with a jerk of his head.

Waverly nodded.

Noah glanced at him, and then locked his gaze on Flaherty as if to say, *Out with it man, I don't have all day.*

"I can see you're quite busy, so, I'll cut to the chase. What sort of relationship did you have with Marion Grand?"

"What? Gentlemen, this is an extremely inopportune time. I do not have the time, nor the inclination to discuss something that is *clearly none of your business.* So, if you will excuse me..." Noah rose and pointed to the door, " ...I believe you can find your way out."

"Mr. Dillow seems to think you may have done away with her," said Flaherty firmly, looking into Noah's eyes without so much as blinking.

Waverly's mouth flew open and he whispered under his breath, *"Great! That was subtle."*

Noah stared at Flaherty for what seemed to Waverly to be an eternity, then sat down and composed his thoughts very carefully, and began to speak in controlled even tones:

"Miss Grand and myself had... *had an arrangement.* She was quite a few years my junior, and I make no apologies, sir, for the way I choose to live my life. But as is often the case, cultural differences between couples in intimate relationships hailing from two different generations sometimes prove insurmountable.

Such was the case with Miss Grand and myself. She left in the dead of the night while I was out of town about two months ago. But not before destroying thousands of pounds worth of equipment, and months of work. *Apparently, purely out of sheer spite.*

Now, that I have had time to think about the situation, I would like to charge Miss Grand with the willful and malicious destruction of my property, and property belonging to the *Cambridge School of Internal Medicine.* Also, I would like to see Miss Grand prosecuted in the highest degree possible for any and all criminal laws she may have broken while in the act of destroying my laboratory."

Flaherty never broke eye contact with Noah and after a long pause asked, "As this happened months ago, why do you come forward now to make this charge? Why not when it happened?"

Noah looked down for a few beats, and then kept his eyes on his desk blotter as he spoke, "I did have an ...well, *an affection* for Miss Grand. I was... I was quite ...upset by what she had done ...maybe the word I'm looking for is *hurt,* by what she had done."

Noah looked up and his features began to harden again as he said, " ...But now, that I've had time to get over the emotional aspects of what she did, I see that it was really a very criminal act. She shredded many important documents and destroyed lab work that will take years to duplicate. As I was very close to a breakthrough in the Leukemia research we were working on, many people may die needlessly as a result of the delay she has caused.

What she has done goes beyond any disagreement she and I may have had. She used her access as my lab manager to enter the laboratory and destroyed valuable, some of it, irreplaceable research, in a juvenile attempt to enact revenge upon me for a petty argument.

Thousands of people will suffer for her little puerile stunt. It's not just a crime against me - *it's a crime against humanity*, and she should be brought to justice."

"That must have been some argument," commented Inspector Waverly.

Noah glared.

"Would you care to share with us the nature of that argument?" asked Flaherty, treading on thin ice.

"I would NOT! I can't believe this. Some emotionally disturbed boy burns down my home. Which by the way, could have been prevented had your department been on the ball. You arrest him, and from the jail cell he accuses ME of murder. Then YOU have the audacity to lend credence to the story by coming into my office and harassing me with personal questions and ludicrous accusations!" thundered Noah.

"Dr. Little..." began Flaherty; retreating slightly, "...We are not accusing you of anything, sir. It was not my intention to anger or upset you. We became aware of a missing person's report on Miss Grand yesterday after interviewing Mr. Dillow. The fact that the cases may in some way be related does not imply any wrong doing on your part.

We merely wanted to speak with you about Miss Grand's disappearance, as you were her last employer and also had the benefit of uh... being the only person in this country to be a known acquaintance. I'm sure you see the logic of beginning our investigation into her disappearance by speaking with you."

"Don't play with that!" Noah exclaimed looking over Flaherty's shoulder at Waverly with great annoyance showing in his face.

Waverly jumped. He had been closely examining the skeleton hanging against the wall on its stand just behind the seated Raymond Flaherty. He had never seen a real human skeleton before. He blushed and looked uncomfortable.

Noah began to speak again as Flaherty turned his gaze from Waverly back to Noah. "Someone just tried to kill me. *Twice!* There is a girl in Mercy Hospital right now because of it. Don't you have more important things to do than go looking for some spoiled brat school girl?"

"Mr. Dillow is already in custody, and has confessed

to the arson of your home and to tampering with your motorcar. Do you have any idea where Miss Grand could be?"

"How should I know?"

"When did you say you had last seen her?"

"Oh... I don't know the exact date. As I said, it was about 2 months ago. It was the day I went to *Dr. Kirby-Smythe's* for the weekend. If you ask him he could probably tell you the exact date. When I returned, she was gone."

"And Dr. Kirby-Smythe is ...?"

"...The head of the Life Sciences Department."

Flaherty made a note on his notepad; *an action which annoyed Noah greatly.*

"I wouldn't be at all surprised if she put young Mr. Dillow up to all of this mischief," said Noah. "...I remember him having quite an obvious infatuation with Miss Grand when the two of them worked together in my stateside laboratory.

Marion must have completely lost her mind. Wrecking my laboratory wasn't enough. She must have sucked poor, impressionable Dillow into her vengeance plans. He would have done anything for her, you know. And I'm sure he was insanely jealous of me. After all, she was sleeping in my bed. I'm sure it wouldn't have taken much to set him off – *seems a good enough motive to me.*

Now, that he's been caught he's making a feeble attempt to use you against me. *Gentleman, it's transparently obvious."*

Flaherty looked at Waverly who nodded slightly, then turned back to Noah. "A similar scenario has been suggested by others."

"Inspector, I am entirely serious when I say I wish to level criminal charges against Marion Grand."

Flaherty rose. "You are certainly at liberty to do so. If you would like to come down to our offices, the magistrate will process the appropriate paperwork."

Noah looked at his watch. "Fine. Expect me within the hour. But fat lot of good it will probably do. I'm sure Marion Grand is getting off an airplane at JFK as we speak."

"Surely, sir, that is not the case," said Flaherty with an icy stare. "...We have spoken at length with the customs authorities at Heathrow Airport. Marion Elizabeth Grand, has NOT left this country... *at least, not under her own power.*

Good day to you, sir."

CHAPTER TWENTY-FOUR

Noah was in a foul mood as he descended the steps leaving the Cambridge Police Department. He had just spent over an hour swearing out the complaint against Marion Grand. It seemed to take an inordinately extended period, especially knowing it was a waste of time - *there was no Marion Grand to find*. He had seen to that. Still, it was important to go through the motions for appearance's sake. Noah was concerned over Flaherty's previous visit. *He knew something*.

Noah went over in his mind all the precautions he had taken. *How could the police pin a murder on him - **there was no body?*** Still, Flaherty kept showing up at Noah's doorstep. *Could Dillow have told him something? But what did Dillow know?* What was more, *what did Dillow have to do with anything?* Todd Dillow had come at Noah straight out of the sun, and had actually tried to kill him twice. *Now, Todd was telling the police that Noah had killed Marion.* It was all very disquieting. Noah knew he had to be very careful.

Noah opened the door of the tan Mercedes and got in. He sat motionless in the driver's seat thinking. *Had he thought of everything? Of course he had.* Let Dillow accuse all he wanted. It didn't matter what Flaherty thought he knew; he couldn't prove anything. The police would never think to look for Marion's remains in such an obvious place - *not in a million years*. Noah was a noted research scientist and taught gross anatomy at one of England's most prestigious medical schools. He was above reproach, and having a skeletal model in his office was no more unusual than a paper clip.

But why was Todd Dillow trying to burn his house down? Well, at least he no longer posed a threat. And with Marion dead, and Dillow in jail, he was safe. He could get back to work on the project. After things had cooled off there was no reason not to believe everything would be back to business as usual. *Weed Killer* would go forward; maybe six months or so behind schedule, but the delay was not significant. He just needed to keep his head and be persistent.

He started to put the key in the ignition but accidently dropped the key ring on the floorboard.

"Shit," he cursed in frustration, then leaned over to pick up the keys. He heard a distant, muffled explosion, like a car backfiring across the street. Then suddenly the driver's side window violently disintegrated, raining glass down on top of him.

*****

"You told me you were goin' to be careful, didn't ya, now?" asked Bob Waverly as he sat down in the chair across from Flaherty's desk.

Flaherty grinned.

"Think it's funny do you? Let's see how funny you think it is when you come flyin' outta the old man's office with a big hole where your ass used to be.

'I'll be subtle' says the man. Then he goes out and tries to pick a fight with a thunderstorm. Are ye daft, man?"

Flaherty frowned. "What was your impression of Little?"

"I think he has no love for you or I, that's for certain."

"I think he's hiding something."

"He's over 50 years old, and he wakes up to find the co-ed he's been bangin' has left him for a younger man. He probably feels a bit silly is all. I don't blame him for not wanting to talk about it."

"You mean Dillow?"

"It's as plain as the nose on your face. Little said he thought our boy had the hots for *Maid Marion;* well, she knew it too. The twist in the thing is what Little probably didn't know was that she didn't want Dillow. But she knew she had him wrapped around her finger, and could tell that Dillow was jealous of Little. She was mad at Little. So, she makes up this crazy germ story and gets Dillow all worked up. Then she just winds him up and aims him at the Professor. He bumps the ole boy off - she gets her revenge, and Dillow goes to jail. Slam bam, thank you ma'am: it's an open and shut."

"Why are you so sure that Miss Grand didn't return Dillow's affections?" asked Flaherty.

"I dunno, Raymond. It's the way he talks about her. I see all this *unrequited love* pent up in the boy," explained Waverly.

"And who are you….*bloody Dear Abby?"* jibbed Flaherty.

"I'm just sayin' is all," responded Waverly with a shrug.

"But how did she know Dillow would get caught?"

"Come on; a dumb ass like *blondie* in there?"

"No, no, Bobby you're really stretching it. She had no way of predicting whether or not Dillow would get caught. And if she didn't want Dillow, and he succeeded in murdering Little, how would she get shed of him?"

"It's not near as hard to swallow as *the germ story."*

"Okay. Try this one. Miss Grand is helping Little do all this strange research and jumps to the wrong conclusions. She gets things all twisted around and really believes that he's out to destroy the world with his super virus.

In her mind she thinks the only way to stop him is to kill him. She believes it so strongly that she figures that she can't afford to fail, so, she writes this letter to Dillow as a back up plan in case she does.

But she loses her nerve, and then goes into hiding. Dillow never hears from her, and decides he has to take her place and stop the mad scientist from destroying the world," theorized Flaherty.

Waverly scratched his head in thought a bit. "Mmm, not bad. That might fly."

"On the other hand..." said Flaherty as he leaned back in his swivel chair and laced his fingers behind his head, "...what if she did try to kill him and failed. You know what a hot head Little can be. What if things got out of hand and he killed her?"

"It would have been self defense," Waverly pointed out.

"Yeah, *but what a scandal.*"

"So, you're saying she tried to kill him, but he killed her in the struggle, and then tried to conceal everything to *avoid the bad press*?"

"*Press* like that would be professional suicide to a man like Little. Either that or he panicked and got in too deep before he knew what he was doing."

"Now, Raymond, it's you who's doing the stretching."

"...Doesn't seem too off the wall to me."

"*...No corpus delicti...*you have no body - no physical evidence whatsoever."

Flaherty sat forward in his chair and placed his chin in his hand. "At least none that we've been able to find.

Waverly raised his eyebrows, pursed his lips, and began to nod his head up and down approvingly. " 'Course, I could swallow everything a lot better if I could see that mysterious journal with my own eyes."

Flaherty frowned. "Dillow says he burned it."

"Damned convenient, that is," said Waverly; his sarcasm showing.

Just then there was a commotion at the other end of the large squad room. Waverly and Flaherty quickly turned to face the disturbance.

A young uniformed policeman burst into the room excited and out of breath. "There's been a shooting!...And out in the car park of the bloody police station!"

*****

Waverly handed Noah a cup of hot tea. Noah's hands were shaking, and small amounts of the dark liquid fell onto the tile floor in front of Flaherty's desk. Waverly put a sympathetic hand to Noah's shoulder and said, "When it rains it pours. Dr. Little, I am so sorry. Thank God you weren't hurt."

If Noah hadn't been so shaken, he probably would have had Waverly for breakfast. He was just too scared to assign blame and adopt his usual adversarial posture - *at least, not at the moment.*

"I thought you people didn't allow guns," said Noah, and then took a loud sip of the hot tea.

Waverly shook his head and leaned up against Flaherty's desk. "It's true that we practice stricter gun control in Great Britain than you do in the United States, but it's not to say that there are no guns. And as in every country, just because something is against the law, doesn't necessarily mean that it is not done."

Raymond Flaherty entered and sat down behind his desk, scowling at his open notepad.

"...Our forensics team has retrieved fragments of a large caliber slug from the lower quadrant of the passenger side door panel of your motorcar," said Flaherty, looking first at Noah, then to Waverly, and back to Noah. "From the angle of entry, the sniper must have fired the shot from one of the upper floors of the building across the street. He undoubtedly used a telescopic sight. We have our men searching the building as we speak. Dr. Little, to be perfectly candid, it is a miracle you are alive, sir. Had you not dropped those keys....?"

"It's Providence, Providence is what it is," chimed Waverly.

"In view of recent events we are considering Marion Grand as a prime suspect," informed Flaherty as he closed his notepad and tossed it atop the desk in front of him, giving Waverly a defeated glance.

Bob Waverly nodded. "Dr. Little, I think you ought to consider allowing us to put you in protective custody."

Noah's heart froze. He knew that Marion was dead. Todd Dillow was in jail. *Who had just tried to shoot him?*

His mind began to race. He didn't know the specific reason why Marion had so turned against him. At first he thought it was because he had blackmailed her, and had treated her so sadistically. Perhaps, he had pushed her too far and she had snapped. *But then there was Dillow.* He hadn't done anything to him, yet he had made two attempts on his life. Noah was baffled as to his motivation. Now, there was a third unknown party trying to assassinate him.

But the paramount concern Noah had was that he might be killed at any moment, and *Weed Killer* was in great jeopardy. True, the project was in its final stages, but with the way things were going, he would not be able to dodge the hail of bullets long enough to finish. And if he died, Noah believed the project, and the world as he knew it, was bound to die with him. His original plan now seemed hopeless. *All at once, he thought of an alternate.*

"No, I will not be held prisoner while the killers are allowed to walk the streets," said Noah defiantly.

"Dr. Little, we are not suggesting that you be held prisoner. It would just be a prudent move to place you in a low profile situation till we've made some headway on the case," said Flaherty.

"Inspector Flaherty, I've had a sample of your department's protection, and quite frankly, I'd just as soon take my chances."

Flaherty visibly deflated from the shot. "Dr. Little, I deeply regret the unfortunate circumstance with the burning of your home, but please believe me when I say Constable Stokes' hesitation in assessing the situation was an isolated incident, and is NOT typical of the procedures adhered to by our department."

"Well, that may be all well and good, but I'd rather you just return my car keys, gentlemen," asked Noah, showing irritation.

Waverly looked at Flaherty with concern.

Flaherty said, "Dr. Little, I'm afraid we can't release your automobile at this time, for it is physical evidence in a felony. I'm sorry, but we have to impound the vehicle till our forensic experts have concluded their examinations. At that time we will be glad to return your motorcar."

Noah was beginning to get angry. "I see. Well, do you suppose you boys could call me a cab?"

The two detectives looked at one another for a long

moment. Then Waverly said, "Dr. Little, I would beg you to reconsider our offer. The person who just shot at you is still at large, and will most assuredly try again."

"Inspector Waverly, I appreciate your concern, but I would appreciate a taxi even more."

The three men sat in a tense silence till Flaherty said, "If that's what you would like," and began to dial the phone on his desk.

CHAPTER TWENTY-FIVE

Noah was profoundly sad as he walked the corridors of the science building for what he knew would be the last time. He unlocked the door to his laboratory and stepped inside. Then he went to the middle of the room and lingered. *This would be the last time he would ever see the inside of a laboratory.* Tonight, Dr. Noah Little planned to exile himself into the culture he so despised, and would never again return to the scholarly aristocracy he so adored.

He removed a plastic bottle of alcohol from a glass cabinet, and then rummaged around various drawers and cabinets till he found a box of cotton balls and a short piece of rubber tubing. He took the collection into his office and sat down at his desk.

Noah unlocked the center drawer of his desk and removed the syringe containing the virus he had once planned to inject into a chimpanzee named *Cheetah*. He held the syringe in his hand for a long time looking at it morosely.

He set the deadly syringe down on the desk in front of him, and then removed his coat, draping it over the back of the swivel chair. He rolled up his sleeve, and then tied the rubber tubing into a tourniquet around his arm. Soon a large blue vein appeared. He moistened one of the cotton balls with the alcohol, and then wiped it over a section of the extended vein. He hesitated. *He had to do this - It was the only way now.*

He pulled the top off the syringe with his teeth and spit the plastic cap onto the floor. He shoved the needle into the vein and injected the virus into his blood stream.

He removed the tourniquet and rolled down his sleeve. *"Funny. I don't feel any different,"* he thought. He moved forward, causing the swivel chair to creak, and tossed the spent syringe into the waste can, then sat back in the chair and stared at Marion Grand's skeleton.

"This is all your fault," Noah said aloud to the skeleton.

The skeleton seemed to stare back at him through the eyeless holes of its skull.

Noah got up and put on his coat. He walked over to the skeleton, stopping in front of it to gaze upon its gruesome face. He turned to leave but stopped short as he reached the door when he heard: *click-a-dee-clack-rattle - rattle-click-click.*

Noah whirled around to face the skeleton. It stood motionless. It just stood there, somehow grinning at him. Noah turned off the light and left.

*****

Noah Little drove his rented automobile into the red-light district of town, and from his car beckoned to the first prostitute he encountered. The couple went to a cheap hotel and had sex. When the sun rose the next morning there were two people infected with Noah's virus - *by the end of that week there were nearly fifty.*

CHAPTER TWENTY-SIX

18 MONTHS LATER

He had had it moved from the billiard parlor almost a year now. Now, the stately grandfather's clock marked time in his study. He hardly ever played billiards anymore. Those days he spent most of his time in his library reading or just sitting behind the enormous rosewood desk listening to the steady: *TICK - TOCK - TICK - TOCK*. He wanted it near. Watching its pendulum gracefully swinging back and forth seemed somehow comforting.

The room, like the man, seemed dry and dusty: a lifeless statue or a monument to something which had once been alive. *TICK - TOCK - TICK - TOCK*. Rows of musty volumes lined the walls on dusty shelves. Books: books filled with dead ideas, written by dead men, whose light had long ago been extinguished from the world. Dry, brittle ideas, yellowing with age, almost as dry and as brittle as the pages on which they were written.

He lived alone now, except for several servants. His wife had died some eight years previous, and his children seldom visited. He had had a granddaughter once. She would have been a doctor. He liked to think she would have been a good one, but she was dead now. *Such a pity.*

The seventy-seven year old Dr. Alec Grand was a mere shell of the man Noah Little had known. But it wasn't the sum of those seventy-seven years which made him such a scarecrow of his former self - it was mostly just the last year and a half. During that time he had aged a lifetime.

"Mr. Mendez to see you, sir," said a man nearly as old as Grand, dressed in a dark three piece suit.

Dr. Grand turned to regard his English butler, Simkins. *Did he have a first name?* Grand couldn't remember it.

"Send him in, Simkins," ordered Grand, and turned back to his clock.

Presently, a swarthy, balding, middle aged Latin man, wearing a blue pin-striped suit and carrying a briefcase sat down opposite Grand.

Alec Grand appeared not to notice the man as he remained mesmerized by the motion of the clock.

TICK - TOCK - TICK - TOCK.

The Latin man made no effort to disturb the aged scientist, just sat patiently, waiting for him to make the first move.

At last Grand turned to the man and asked hoarsely, "You have news?"

"He's left Africa," answered the man in perfect English, with just the slightest hint of an accent. " ... He withdrew a large amount of money from his bank account via a wire transfer from a bank in New York City. We have operatives trying to trace his movements from there."

Grand made no response.

"Mr. Dillow's legal fees continue to escalate. I am afraid his outlook is not very promising. Do you wish to keep his lawyer on retainer?"

"...Yes."

"Of course, the decision is yours, but it seems to me, with all due respect, to be a waste of a whole lot of money."

"Perhaps, but I feel a moral obligation to Mr. Dillow."

"As you wish, sir."

TICK - TOCK - TICK - TOCK.

"I suppose you're here for money," commented Grand dryly.

Mendez nodded affirmatively.

"It seems I'm paying a great deal of money for very little results."

"Dr. Little has proved a lot more... how should I say... *slippery*, than we would have believed. He rarely stays any place over a week. He has access to almost unlimited funds to finance his travels, and therefore changes countries almost as frequently as he does cities. And he often goes to countries off the beaten path so to speak, like Chad and Algeria.

He also seems to have a sixth sense that warns him when we're near. It's rather uncanny. In addition to the near misses at Cambridge and Frankfurt, we did manage to graze him in Johannesburg.

But I assure you, Dr. Grand, we are very close now. It won't be long."

Grand stared at Mendez for an uncomfortable interval, and then took out his checkbook. "I certainly hope so, Mr. Mendez. Please keep in mind that your associates are not the only ones in this line of work. I'm interested in results - *not near misses*. If your, uh... firm can't handle the job, I shall employ those who can. I've heard of an Italian concern which is quite adept at resolving things of this nature."

Mendez looked down, avoiding Dr. Grand's electric stare.

TICK - TOCK - TICK - TOCK.

Grand wrote a check for seventy-five thousand dollars and handed it to Mendez as he said, "I look forward to a favorable report in the immediate future."

Mendez took the check, stood, smiled wanly nodding his farewell, and left the room.

TICK - TOCK - TICK - TOCK.

Grand looked down at the notebook in front of him. He opened the book and flipped through its pages. The hand was so familiar to him. Long, long ago he had read those same strokes on test papers. The words written on the ruled lines: that of a genius; his best student; a friend even; *almost a son.*

So many things he had read in those notes were just too familiar, *painfully familiar.* They were *his words* more than they were Noah Little's. *He knew he had been the one who had created the monster.*

When he had reached the end of the journal, he removed a letter that had been tucked between its pages, and reread for more than the hundredth time, the hand written paragraphs of someone else's cursive that he found also *painfully familiar:*

"Dear Papa,

I've asked a good friend of mine, Todd Dillow, to send this book to you. Please read it carefully and take whatever steps your conscience leads you to take. If you are reading these words, I have failed, and Todd is trying to finish what I've started. If he fails, the responsibility falls to you.

It pains me to have to tell you this, but Noah Little is planning to unleash a plague unparalleled in all of history to destroy people whom you have taught him to hate. I know it was not your intention to send him down this dark road, but regardless of what you meant, your words have inspired him to become the judge, jury and executioner of the human race.

I know this sounds bizarre, but read this journal and you will see. You're a scientist; you will understand. You are also enough of a psychologist, and you know Noah Little well enough to know that he believes what he has written, and will do exactly what is outlined in his journal. Nothing short of death will stop him. He must not succeed.

If you are reading this, I am either in jail as a murderess, or an attempted murderess ... or dead. Papa, I will not explain my reasons. As you read Noah's words, you will see why I did what I have done. If I've failed, and Noah still lives, and Todd chooses to take my place - help him Papa. If he fails - succeed him.

Love,

Marion"

CHAPTER TWENTY-SEVEN

The music from the doorbell chimed through the large house. Marie Little woke from her nap and sat up on the plush sofa. The doorbell sounded again. She rose and walked through the exquisitely furnished mansion, headed for the front door.

Marie had kept her married name. *Why, she did not exactly know.* Maybe it was because she had liked being *Mrs. Noah Little.* There was a sort of respect and notoriety that went along with the title. She had become accustomed to it, and it had not ended with the divorce decree.

She had held up well. Despite her age of 48 years, she was an extremely attractive woman. There were a few lines around her eyes, she colored her hair every now and then, and her large breasts were not quite as pert as they had been in her younger days, but she could still turn heads with the best of them.

The doorbell chimed again.

"I'm comin', I'm comin'," she said to the closed door.

She grasped the doorknob, turned it, and opened the door. When she beheld her visitor, her mouth fell open and she stood there stupefied.

Noah Little was tanned and lean. All and all, he looked better fit than she had seen him in years, although there was a sort of weariness in his eyes. He wore khaki pants and a tan shirt with no coat, as he stood at her threshold carrying a suitcase.

"Hello, Marie," said Noah, and forced a sly grin.

Marie closed her mouth and her green eyes narrowed with anger. "Did you know that there was a warrant out after you, buster?!"

Noah raised his eyebrows and shrugged his shoulders. "No... I can't say as I did. Uh, what for?"

"What for?!!" Marie exclaimed, and looked up at the ceiling. "I can't believe it. He asked me, 'What for?'" She looked back at him. "You know damn well what for! You haven't made a single alimony payment in almost two years!"

"Oh, that. Well, I'm sorry. Aren't you going to ask me in?"

Marie stared at him in disbelief. "What?" said she, and began to shake her head, then made a grand sweeping gesture for him to enter. "Why not."

Noah was tired. He had flown in from JFK that afternoon after being back in the United States only fourteen hours. Since he had left England, he had hit most of the countries in Europe and a fair number of those on the continent of Africa. Three days previous he had left Algeria for the United States, and during the brief layover in New York, withdrew an extremely large amount of money from one of his bank accounts, then packed the money into three worn suitcases, one of which he now tossed onto an ottoman in Marie's living room.

He popped the latches and opened the suitcase, revealing it to Marie's astonished eyes, to be crammed full of one hundred dollar bills.

"One hundred and fifty thousand dollars... Sorry it was so late... been travelin' you see. This should catch things up and have me paid ahead a little. I hope the delay didn't cause you any serious inconvenience."

Marie beheld the treasure with transparent avarice. She fondled the top layer of notes, then closed the case and said with a bemused grin on her face, "Oh... well, no. Uh... no serious inconveniences. Uh, won't you sit down... uh would you...?" She smiled. "... Like a drink?"

Noah smiled broadly. *He was enjoying this.*

"Why thank you, Marie, that would be lovely," he

said as he plopped down onto the sofa.

She returned with two drinks in hand, and then gave one of them to Noah as she sat down on the couch beside him.

"Scotch and soda, right?"

"You remembered."

"Of course, I remembered."

Noah looked down the low cut frock at her ample cleavage, *and he also began to remember a few things.*

"You really look good, Marie."

"You really think so?" asked Marie with a bashful smile, while she absently twisted one of her long red locks.

"Yeah. Real good," answered Noah undressing her with his eyes. He took a sip from the scotch.

"You say you've been traveling. Where did you go?"

"England, Germany, France, Italy, India, and even several countries in Africa. I saw everything from Buckingham Palace to the Pyramids."

"Wow! That really sounds exciting."

Noah shrugged and took another sip of his drink.

"Did Marion go with you?" asked Marie as her features began to harden.

Noah did not answer at first, then said, "Part of the way - at the beginning... Marion and I... well, there isn't a Marion and I anymore".

Noah took another sip from the scotch and looked very sad for a moment, and Marie actually caught herself feeling sorry for him.

"But enough about me. Looks like you've done all

right for yourself here, Marie," said Noah, looking around the room admiringly. "... The place looks great."

Marie looked surprised.

"You always did have good taste," said Noah as he continued to look around, nodding his head up and down approvingly.

"I thought... Well, I always thought you hated the things I bought."

Noah seemed thoughtful for a few seconds, then set the drink down on the coffee table and looked deep into her eyes.

"Marie, I was always too busy with my work to appreciate the home you made for me. I've always been that way. I've never been able to realize a good thing when I had it."

Their eyes locked. When the silence became uncomfortable, Noah took out a cigarette and lit up.

Marie's eyes widened. "When did YOU take up smoking?"

"Oh... I dunno. Not long ago."

"I don't believe this: *Mister Treat Thy Body as a Temple?*"

"*Humph.* I just woke up one morning and I realized, *Hey! We're all gonna die.* What the hell." said Noah darkly as he watched the smoke float in front of him.

"Can I have one?" asked Marie.

"Sure," answered Noah and gave her a cigarette.

Marie put the cigarette in her mouth, and Noah lit it with his lighter. He flipped the lighter closed with a loud click, then reached out to Marie's face, and gently stroked her cheek with his thumb, index, and middle fingers, still holding the lighter with his ring finger and pinkie. She could feel his soft touch, and the cold steel of the lighter. Marie closed her eyes for an instance, seemingly enraptured.

Noah put his cigarette in the ashtray. Marie suddenly opened her eyes. He took hers from her hand, and placed it in the ashtray beside his, then held her hand inside his own. She looked confused. He moved slowly closer, then gently kissed her on the lips, and withdrew to study her reaction. She was stunned, and just sat there blinking. He kissed her again, this time longer and harder.

Marie began to reciprocate. She placed her hand on his cheek, and then ran it along the side of his face into his hair. Noah inserted his tongue into her mouth and began to lean forward, pushing her down slightly into the corner of the sofa. "*What am I doing?*" she thought to herself, and began to make a muffled sound in protest, then pushed him back roughly.

She was about to let him have it when she stopped herself. She was surprised by what she saw. *He just sat there looking at her... with tears rolling down his cheeks!* She had never seen him cry before. No, that wasn't true, she remembered one other time. *He had cried when Mandy died.*

She wiped a tear from his cheek. He softly took her hand to his lips and began to kiss her fingertips. More tears fell. He reached for her other hand, and then held both of them in his lap while he spoke.

"You were the only one whoever cared and I treated you like shit. Marie, I'm so sorry. I thought I knew it all, but now, I see that I don't know anything.

Marie looked at his earnest face as absolution began to swell in her heart.

"I've changed, you know. I can see so clearly now. Everyone I trusted has stabbed me in the back. You were the only one who stuck by me.

I don't know. I've heard about people having a mid-life crisis. Maybe that's what it was. Maybe I thought the grass would be greener on the other side. I don't know. All I know is that I've traveled the whole world looking for the treasure that I threw away out of my own ignorance.

Every night I'd fall asleep in some hotel room in one of the four corners of the earth, and the last conscious thought I'd have would be of your face. I have lots and lots of money. I can have anything in the world, but I threw away the only thing I ever truly wanted... *and that was you*. And things ... don't mean a flyin' flip without you...without you - I have nothing."

At this point Marie's eyes were wet and misty, and her lower lip was beginning to tremble.

Noah looked at her with pain showing in his eyes and said almost in a whisper, "... *Marie, I love you.*

That done it.

Marie Little pounced on her ex-husband with *the passion of an escaped convict.* Fifteen minutes later Marie was straddling a nude Noah Little while waves in the water bed made a muffled sloshing sound. Then she bounced up and down moaning with sexual ecstasy. Noah's semen erupted into Marie's body at the exact moment she came violently. She screamed and convulsed side to side sending her long red hair flying in all directions. She made soft mewing sounds as she began to ride up and down on his shaft more slowly. She looked down at Noah, smiling with orgasmic delight. Noah gripped her hips a little tighter and smiled with satisfaction.

As her climax began its decrescendo Noah absently focused on the way her breasts rived up and down in unison as she rocked up and down, and back and forth. He didn't know the exact number; he had lost track somewhere along the way, but had been with over a hundred different women in the past 18 months. He began to marvel at their diversity. A woman's breasts were almost like fingerprints - no two pair were alike. There were so many variables in size, shape, texture and the configuration of the nipples. *"It was truly amazing,"* he thought.

The next morning he watched the sun shine down onto the sleeping form of Marie Little as he buttoned his shirt. Noah smiled. She looked so peaceful. She was completely oblivious to the ticking time bomb he had planted inside her body the night before.

Flowing through the veins of every prostitute he had slept with through his worldwide sexual odyssey was a virus that would one day awaken and claim their lives. Not only would it claim their lives, but the lives of all that had slept with them, and all those who had slept with the ones who had slept with them. There were now thousands of unwary carriers of *Noah Little's child - a virus created by his own hand,* and that was now even a part of his own flesh and blood, which he passed on in an unholy copulation. Noah had become the *Johnny Appleseed of Death* – now, his seed had been planted in yet another fertile field.

Noah looked down at Marie one last time. *He hated her.* Now, he had his revenge, and it tasted sweet.

He pointed his finger at the blissfully slumbering figure as if it were a gun. He worked his thumb up and down as if it were the hammer and said, "Bang! ... Gotcha!"

Then Noah began to chuckle softly to himself and did so all the way to the street.

CHAPTER TWENTY-EIGHT

Derelict Noah Little removed his hands from Lavonne's neck. The naked prostitute turned to face him and said, "Thanks, you give a great massage."

Noah nodded and grinned sheepishly.

"... And Happy Birthday."

Noah repeated his response.

Five minutes later Noah lay on his bed smoking a cigarette while he watched Lavonne dress. When she was fully clothed, she headed for the door, but paused with her hand on the knob, and turned back to Noah.

"I really had a good time," said Lavonne. " ... Maybe we can get together again sometime."

Noah took a drag off the cigarette and exhaled loudly. "Who knows. You know what they say - *anything is possible.*"

Lavonne looked at the strange man for a lingering moment, then left, closing the door behind her. When she hit the street she was overwhelmed with an almost ubiquitous feeling of depression. She couldn't explain it. It was like something her mother used to say: *"I feel like someone just walked over my grave."* She had time to turn at least one more trick, but went straight home instead. She was just too sad to be around anyone.

Noah stood at the window watching Lavonne cross the street, and then as she disappeared down the sidewalk. He took the last draw off his cigarette and crushed it out in an ashtray sitting on the window sill. He began to whistle *Beethoven's Fur Elise,* and continued to whistle the same tune as he showered and dressed. He put on clean underwear, but the same pants and shirt. Once he was dressed, he happily skipped down the stairs, through the lobby of the cheesy hotel and back onto the streets.

He felt pretty good. He could plant one more seed tonight. So, he was off to find another whore.

As he walked along he began to smile to himself. He had accomplished his destiny. It had been a long hard road, and not exactly the road he thought he was to travel, but he felt confident that he had spread the virus over a wide enough area to prevent the devolution of the human race, and save society. It seemed a shame though. No one would ever know of his great sacrifice. No statues would ever be erected in his honor. The children of the future which he had saved would not read in their history books about the great Noah Little, and about how he single handedly saved the human race. *They wouldn't know... but he would, and that would be enough.*

A tall Hispanic man walking the opposite way along the busy sidewalk bumped into Noah. Suddenly, a sharp pain detonated in Noah's kidney, and then ripples of agony ran the length of his torso like a stone dropped into a small placid pond.

Hector Mendez's operative pulled the bloody knife from Noah's side, then dropped it into his suit coat and continued down the sidewalk unnoticed, hardly even breaking his stride.

At first Noah just froze in his tracks, and then he slowly sank to his knees. People on the sidewalk stopped to look. Then Noah toppled over onto his face. A black man rolled him over onto his back. By now the whole side of his tan shirt was covered in blood. Somewhere a woman screamed.

Noah looked up at the glow of a street light. The corners of his vision began to blur. He was aware of a lot of commotion going on around him, but could not make out any details. He abruptly became very cold, and all sound and sight of his mortal life began to mix with that of his eternal one. It was all very confusing, and he couldn't recognize anything until from the afterlife came a sound he knew:

Click-de-clack-rattle-rattle-click-click.